Leighton Park
School

MIRABA

A collection of stories from the amazing world of Miraba; a spiritual world of the imagination, constructed like layers of an onion, where a central, colour-changing sun pours out its energy on a kingdom of twin rulers, the Soferei.

DREAMCATCHERS PUBLISHING

Ken Sullivan
Leighton Park School
Shinfield Road,
Reading,
Berkshire. RG2 7ED
UK

Photocopying and electronic copying or storage is permitted for educational purposes. Dreamcatchers is a non-profit making venture, generously supported by the Leighton Park School Parent-Teacher Association.

Published September 2011

ISBN: 978-0-9566473-3-7

The imaginery world of Miraba is a construction of Ben Singer and Jeremy Rishton, of Leighton Park School Creative Writing Group.

The stories, illustrations and articles of this imprint are written by the Leighton Park School Creative Writing Group, and are set within the boundaries of the imaginary world. This is a community writing project, co-owned by the authors and illustrators listed below:

Jonah Arend	Jeremy Rishton
Sophie Bogner	Blake Simons
Jake Cyriax	Ben Singer
Alistair Dunstan	Acadia Stanton
Michael Hawkins	Ken Sullivan
Naomi Holloway	Ben Twineham

Thanks and acknowledgement to Sergon for the use of his sea monster illustration.

Recommended price £5.50

Printed in Reading, Berks by CONSERVATREE Print & Design, Units 4a and 4b Paddock Road, Caversham, Reading,   RG4 5BY

Introduction

Despite what you might assume, this book does not originate on Earth. This is a record of tales passed to us by the power of the spirit world via the Eidolons of the Upper Realm (aka Ben Singer and Jeremy Rishton), into the humble pens of the (generally, but not exclusively, human) authors previously listed. We cannot apologise for what is not our doing. Our mission is not to educate, entertain or inform, merely to be the conduit of these stories.

If this is really not your thing then, to coin a Miraban phrase: "you are well off the force line!" If you are not one of us, then you must close this book now and put it down. Walk away from it, without a backward glance! It is not for you. We apologise for wasting your moment.

However,

If you are one of us, then......

WELCOME TO MIRABA.

This book is dedicated to the dynamic group of young people at Leighton Park School who spent Tuesday afternoons arguing back and forth the fine detail of the world of Miraba.

Many thanks to Chris Routh, librarian, for hosting us, for her tolerance and encouragement.

Best wishes to Jake Cyriax, one of our founding members, and Jonah Arend, as they move on to new challenges.

CONTENTS

Force line

Force line

Frost claw

Rockies

capitol

Fertile
lands
majic

Kings
Road

(South)
west
planes

Force
line

Twin cities
(first king from)
Great bridge + Statu
majic

Force
line

4

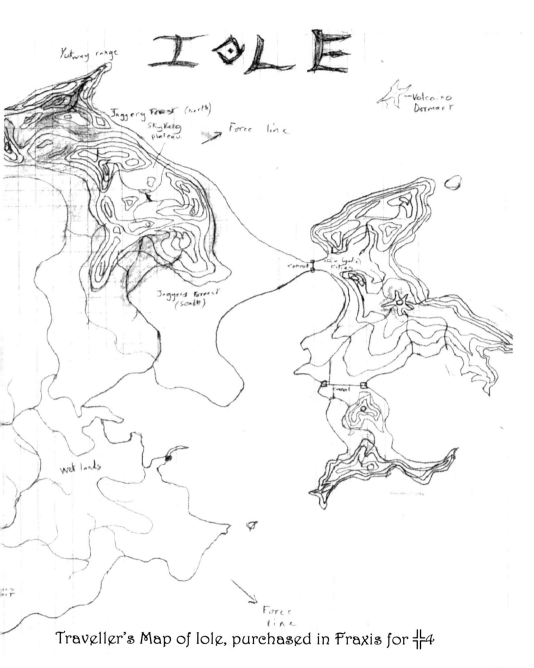

IOLE

Yutway range

Jaggery Forest (North)

SkyKarg plateau

→ Force line

Volcano Dormant

control Iole (gate) ridge

Jaggery Forest (South)

control

Wet lands

Force line

Traveller's Map of Iole, purchased in Fraxis for ₶4

5

Service Recruit

"Every city dreams of it's own destruction."
Amjad Rafi, Scholar of Planar Imprints

So there I was, swinging from the ceiling and facing a certain very armed, quite angry lady who, from the look of things, was planning to kill me.

It was not the best of days.

"Well," she said, "I do have to ask what were you expecting to get out of this?"

My mouth answered before my brain could interfere. "Money," it said, and I privately cursed my traitorous organ.

She smiled and crossed her arms. It sounded like it was a nice movement, but it wasn't. "And were you expecting to get away with it?"

"Well, I was, kind of, Ma'am." I said. My body swung lazily in the draft, and I tried to shift the balance to my right. Nevertheless, my mouth carried on. "Otherwise, I wouldn't have done it, really," I said, and winced.

"Ah-hum." The smile of the woman was getting every bit thinner and thinner by the moment, and it threatened to not become a smile at all but a grimace, or possibly a sneer. "You wouldn't mind telling me who swore you that oath of honesty, would you?"

I opened my mouth, but she must have known what I was thinking, or that something flippant was coming, because she cut me off with a "Shut up, tell me!"

"Um, it was me, me, me," I said. I wriggled my free foot in the air. This movement caused me to swing a bit more to the left. "I swore it to myself, as it were. Still binding."

Others may say oaths aren't binding unless you swear them on the spirits, but I say different. Oaths are oaths, and sanctions like that aren't to be taken lightly, of any kind. The woman made a little noise with her mouth, "H-um," it went. She nodded and frowned. "And is there any other reason you won't stop talking, little girl? It just gets you in trouble." Another one of those smiles. Gods, those were really getting frightening.

"I just kinda like talking," I said, "and speaking. I get speaky when I'm nervous," I explained.

I guess I should tell you at this moment just what was going on, and why was so jumpy about everything. I was currently hanging from the ceiling with my left foot rather painfully entangled in my scarf, and I was pretty sure that it was cutting off all the blood. There was a hole in the roof and the sunlight was streaming through the hole like the universe's ironic blessing, warming my scales. The way these two things are linked is that I was on the roof there when it broke through, my scarf got caught on a snag and wrapped around my foot and literally left me hanging in front of the woman whose house I was trying to burgle. The woman who was the local crime lord of this district was standing in front of me with her weapon-spirits and a very deadly look on her face, and I was not feeling too pleased right then. I hated my luck.

"Is there a reason why you're a lizard-god?" she asked.

I shook my head, causing the scarf holding me up to wobble. "Nothing in particular. Is there a reason you've got spirit-weapons?"

She frowned and crossed her arms again. Let me tell you, in case you haven't seen anyone with that many weapons fold both arms at once, it was pretty impressive. There was all sorts of action and folding going on there, getting them in the right order so that they overlap just right, so they give the impression of an impenetrable wall of steel, with elbows peeking out at you from the corner. It's very good for intimidating guys, or at least guys like me.

"Some minor spirit?" I guessed, "A household goddess of menial labour going rouge, bound to your swords? You're not the first to try that."

She grimaced and spat. That was surprising, given how neatly she'd acted otherwise. People here didn't tend to do anything that messed up their own abode, even if they broke free of their normal places of bondage. But given that I'd crashed in here through the rooftop, perhaps she figured a little bit of saliva wouldn't make much of a difference beneath the rubble. "Better than some sage-less tramp," she swore. "You're not getting out of here."

"Actually," I said, and reached for the dagger.
I'd been swinging myself hard enough to get the momentum to reach the table – for quite some time. Irritating her was only a way of distracting her from my true intentions and, quite honestly, having a bit of fun meanwhile. My right hand picked up the dagger and fumbled it: a frantic swing with my left caught it. I saw the woman open her mouth in surprise, and then focus it into a shape that would direct some Command Word – something that, if I was unlucky, would rip the dagger from my hand or through it and into hers.

I didn't waste any time and continued the movement of my hand, twisting my body around into a spine-cracking shape until I could finish the curve and cut through my silken scarf. I dropped painfully on the edge of a piece of rubble and raised a small cloud of dust, just at the same time as I saw a remarkably small axe pass through the space I was just in and hit the nearby wall. I staggered up, coughing, and saw her mouth just end framing those mystic words that would undoubtedly unleash carnage and bloody vengeance upon me .

"Men! To me!"
Ah, well. Maybe it was something more mundane. But undoubtedly just as effective.

I dived for the box on the table – the only unornamented, undecorated box, vain bitch – grabbed it and barrelled past my captor. She was ready for an attack but not an escape, and I

9

darted past, unmarked apart from a lost lock of my hair. Vindictively, I kicked back and heard something click — I think it was her ankle, from the satisfying yell she made and the way her pace stuttered. The guards were coming, but it did not matter now.

My feet were off her wooden floor and touching the stones of the city, running on the city, through the city, with the city. The cobblestones breathed through me and I took encouragement from them, dreams from them, directions from them, and I turned a sharp left and jumped up the wall for the handhold I knew was there, I sensed was there, I could not but feel was there.

There was not even a pause, as my fingers grasped the stone: they flung me up and I swung my other arm to catch the rooftop and use the momentum to swing me over. There was what might have been the sound of arrows hitting earth is behind me, but there was no time to worry about that now or to catch my breath. My feet sung to me about escape, mere seconds away.

I ran till my breath was torn out of me, and my legs complained and my hand trembled and the shouts grew louder and closer, but I was no longer worried: the ground beneath me rattled with the terrible sound of an approaching machine. I was counting under my breath.

"One, two, three, four, go now," I jumped.

I floated in the air for a moment, it seemed, just before I landed with a clatter of my bones. The timing was perfect. The train, a beautiful beast of stone and metal, joined and welded together, burst underneath me in mid-air and rocketed its way along the fault-line that goes through the centre of this city and carried me away to safety, or at least to relative safety, where people weren't shooting at me.

My feet trembled on the edge, the drop that goes down to the passenger cabins, but I righted myself and managed to steady myself on the coach. I panicked for a moment until I felt the solid wood of the box tucked under my arm. Grinning, I got it out and looked at it, preparing for a moment before opening it, and then my side jerked like it had just been punched by a bull and I tumbled down to the passenger compartment, my theft slipping from my fingers. In the moment between when I hit the ground and before the train sped off, I thought I saw an archer on the edge of one of the slum's rooftops, his bow undrawn and the arrow piercing through my side like a broken rib. There was a concerned face in front of me, but it was not important.
"The box..." I asked, and he looked behind him for a moment and then shook his head. I was numb. I couldn't feel much.

It's just not fair.

Amjad turned the box over in his hands, and then back over again. There was nothing that marked it as unusual or dangerous, which was often the case with these things. He felt it rather irritating and un-dramatic. In the bed he was sitting on, the girl turned in her sleep and gave a groan. Amjad wondered if she dreamt of cities too.
"What are you going to do with her?"

Amjad turned to the woman who had asked the question and flashed her his very best, quiet smile, as dry as the Nomad's Path and about as friendly. "I was thinking to employ her," he said.

The woman snarled and would've crossed her arms had she not already done so when she came in. "That box is mine," she said, "and that girl is a thief."

"Says the murderer," said Amjad, and watched the woman raise her hand in anger and drop it back down as soon as his gaze centred on her. "She stole from a crime lord and –almost- made it out on her own. I'd say that makes her a good prospect, wouldn't you?"

The woman spat to the side, and Amjad absently reached over his foot and rubbed out the mark she'd just made in the carpet. "And what will your colleagues suspect when they find a young girl sleeping in your bed?" she asked.

"Nothing," Amjad chuckled and looked down at the subject of their conversation, "my colleagues know how my tastes run. Perhaps if she wasn't a woman..."
He looked at her and smiled. It was always enjoyable watching her work herself into a rage and to have to force herself back down. "Degenerate!" she spat.

"But it is quite enjoyable," Amjad said, "you should really widen your views, Madame. What matters it, if a man lies with another man?"

The woman flinched at such a direct reference, and only just recovered enough to grimace her lips into a snarl. Amjad chuckled. "I tolerate you and your criminal acts because you are supposed to report technology like this to me."

He tapped the box on the edge of the desk, and she winced. "Don't worry, it's empty," he said, "but I'd advise you move now. Perhaps the guards will be receiving information on you now, since you are no longer proving trustworthy to me."

The woman's hands fell easily to her twin hammers, fingers resting lightly on the hilts.
"Oh, do try that!" Amjad said, pleasantly. "I've wanted a chance to take you down myself ever since I met you. Unluckily, the service doesn't like me exposing myself like that," he shrugged, "but in self-defence, it couldn't be helped."

The woman drooped, her anger gone and her energy with it. She gave a small sneer, but her heart wasn't in it. Looking at the bed, she frowned. "What do you want with her?"

Amjad held the box up. "This," he said, "could define the course of this city. She would've sold it elsewhere." He looked down at the figure dozing gently on the bed, and smiled. "She could have decided on the course of countries."

There was no response from the woman.

"She dreams of cities through her sleep, and speaks to them when she's awake. Did you see the way she ran?" Amjad let out a breath of joy. "No normal human could run like that. She knew

where she was going, every step of the way, every bump and jump and roof and stone, all to that one jump in the sunrise." He looked down. "She was an orphan, you said? She grew up in the city, lived in it, breathed it her whole life. The spirits of this place love her, Madame, and help her. That fact, combined with her intelligence, her daring, her desperation to steal this...."
the box came up held in his fingers again "....could lead to one of the best operatives we've ever seen."

He looked at the woman, a condescending smile on his lips. "Go rule your little world, Madame!" he said, "I've got better games to play."

Amjad had escorted the woman out and hid the box and made some food and some drink and was waiting with it at the edge of his bed when the girl woke up.
The first thing she said was "Wuh?"

Amjad smiled and pressed the meal into her hands, and let her eat a bit. It was quite amusing to watch something so finely cooked disappear so fast, and it had a calming effect on him. Briefly, he wondered what it would be like to have children. Well, that was a useless question anyway. He had more important matters to focus on now. The girl finished her plate, with the priorities of any street rat, then looked up at him and sniffed and grabbed at his hair. Bemused, Amjad let her. It was, he recalled, a subculture of the eastern immigrants. Or was it west?
Then she looked up at him and said "Who're you?"

"It's Amjad Rafi, for now," Amjad smiled and took the plate from her and then the cup and arranged them neatly on top of each other. "I'm a scholar at the moment, and a quite good one, too. So in a moment, I'll ask your name, and then we'll be talking about the dreaming of cities, but first- what do you know about The Service?"

The girl looked up. Her mouth worked slowly. Finally she said, "But what could I offer them?"
The spirits of the city above, Amjad knew, on the level where only mages and strange men with mad eyes dared enter – they loved this girl. They helped her to taunt harm, gave her luck good and bad, as was their will. To think what she could do with some training!

Amjad smiled. "Quite a lot," he said.

The Bowl

The Soferex Sinistra, one of the great kings of Iole, arguably the most powerful country in the whole of Miraba, played with the traditional Iolian world bowl that sat on his desk. The ancient tribes of his country, seeing the horizon stretching away until it curved up and met the sky, had inferred that the world was shaped like a bowl, an endless sky stretching above it with the sun positioned above the very centre of the world, which was, of course, them.

Long after the invention of long-distance sea-travel had proved these primitive musings wrong - showing the world to be the inside of a huge sphere, the sun fixed in the middle and fading from one end of the spectrum to the other, going out at night and giving out nothing but the deadly rays known to cause the most terrible cancers and mutations - the tradition of the elegantly carved bowls remained. On the inside was carved a crude map of Iole, in the rough style of the ancients, but the outside was coated in glass, representing how the world was, as indeed all worlds were, utterly transparent from the outside.

That reminded him to get a servant to fetch the complete set out again, the concentric layers stacked on top of each other, representing the worlds below and the worlds above. Looking at the bowl again, he saw that, although of high quality, it couldn't possibly be hand-made; far more likely that the craftsman had been schooled in the art of shifting, and had transported his soul and his raw materials to create the bowl, and that the heightening action of the planes above caused a bounty of the things to appear in the living world.

The worlds above were all-important to a ruler in his age. The ancient spirits, those of the dead ancestors of modernity, who controlled the tides and the winds and made sure that Iole remained powerful and prosperous before all other countries, were starting to fade; being absorbed by the entropic nature of those places close to the sun. The secrets of spirit-making had been lost, and so, as the main weapon of Iole faded to flat, white uniformity, the world was in turmoil. It was all-important to research new methods of control, new magics that would keep their iron fist on the world tightly clenched.

His heart started to beat faster with the adrenalin of power, as the sun outside started to change from turquoise to light blue, and the servants drew the blinds to protect the inhabitants from the burning rays that the great sphere emitted during the late evening. However, this was also the best time of day to be social in the low lands, full of valleys and far away from the terrible orb. The Soferex's wife entered the room, body covered up with an impenetrable but tightly clinging dress, dark gloves pulled up to her shoulders to protect her from the sky-fire.

The Soferex got up and made similar preparations, allowing a nearby servant to pull up his socks and apply his gloves. He had heard that up in the mountains they covered themselves with sticky ant-grease at night to protect against the stronger sun that burned up there, and felt a faint pang of disgust. He followed his wife down to the doorway, where they put on their veils and opened up their parasols, the fearful blue of the sun probing their evening protection.

Surf The Great Tail

Are you thinking of 'going extreme' for your next spirit day?

Already hiked across the West Planes?

Have you fought sharks in the Deep Blue of midnight?

Think you've experienced it all? Think again!

This season, try riding the waters of the Great Tail, whose walls of water are as high as the Gem Exchange Tower! Fifteen percent survival rate guaranteed.

Sentimental? Buy necklaces for your loved ones, made from wagga shells (buy all gifts before you surf, and we'll guarantee delivery, in case of death).

Can you out-surf the sea monsters and avoid the stinging claws of the grabfish? Probably not, but it's fun to try and a great way to die.

Survived? If you want to relax a little more, then chill out on the multicoloured sands of Equinox Beach, where flying whales can be regularly seen.

Warning: contact with the sands for more than two hours can cause corrosive skin damage. Death or permanent disability is likely to affect anyone surfing the Great Tail. Terms and conditions apply. All holiday insurance is void.

Wish you were here.

The Day of Mystica

Gorda and Moogan stood on the cliff top, looking east.

"Do you believe in the spirits?"

The silence seemed to deepen, after Moogan had said it. It was as if the rocks and the air were listening for the answer. The rocks and the brown sand of the planes unrolled into the distance, where red peaks peered lazily over the horizon. It was the public holiday of Mystica, when normal life was put on hold, and the people of the towns and villages of the Edge explored their spiritual beliefs.

" 'I know nothing of what I cannot see and cannot touch.' My mother said that to me. If you cannot see it or touch it, then it either cannot be there or it cannot count for much. It is all superstition," said Gorda, without deviating from her faraway stare at the red mountains. Then she remembered something else and smiled, "Do you know my grandmother sings to the spirits before bed, every night."

The two girls chuckled, covering their mouths with their ample sleeves. It was not polite to laugh at an elder, even behind her back. They felt guilt at their emotion.

Moogan continued in a whisper, hardly daring to say what she was thinking, "My grandfather...he speaks to the trees...," she dissolved in mirth, no longer pretending, "and he speaks to the river, and he waits and listens for an answer."

It was too much. They laughed until tears were in their eyes, and the sleeves were again of use in drying the sides of their noses. And then they fell into a reflective silence.

"Does the river answer?" asked Gorda, breaking the spell with wistful interest. Despite her joking, she still hoped for the spirit world to show itself to her, some day.

They looked out, together, across the vastness of dust and parched, weathered rock. The enormity of it silenced them again. Their hands touched and they entwined fingers, as friends do when there is nothing to say.

High above, a songbird hovered on fragile wings and sang an intricate melody. It rose and fell, rose and fell again, like a human voice repeating a message over and over,
"Here I am, right before you. Here I am, right before you."

But, all they heard was the wind blowing the dust from the east, which formed into little devils and hurt their eyes, forcing them to squint and wash out the grit with protective tears.

The Guncjan

He couldn't help looking. It was just too hilarious. There was this tubby, plump-looking man having a very close look at the display on a stand, heaving with cheap cloth, fake jewellery and artificial pottery. He was having such a close look that his nose hovered only centimetres in front of earthenware formed into a shapeless object. He could only identify it, with much imagination, as a vase after having looked at it for the third time. The man was about a foot smaller than the local, with a retreating hairline, streaked with grey, and friendly wrinkles around his eyes. Rhanas saw him inquiring the price from the vendor, who wore a mask of friendly politeness on his weathered face and who named an amount almost triple the normal selling price.

The other man smiled serenely, pushed back his glasses and started rummaging through his large rucksack. At this point Rhanas couldn't help himself. I He pushed himself from the wall on which he was leaning in the shade and walked over.
"Oy, Renésch!" he called out.

 The vendor looked up. A look of hostility crept into his eyes and he drew back a little.
"Make it three," he said. The tourist looked up, surprised.

"Ten," the vendor answered.

"Four."

"Six," he offered hesitantly.

"Make it four or I'll make sure you lose a customer," Rhanas said slowly, nodding towards the man with the rucksack staring at him with his mouth slightly open.

The vendor leaned over the stall so that only the other could hear his whispered words.
"The business with the tourists is one of our best sources of income. Who do you think you are, Rhanas?"

Smiling, Rhanas stepped back, looking calmly into his furious face and at all the surrounding stalls from which there were many evil glances shot in his direction.
"We all know the decree of the Soferex. Foreign guests – tourists - are to be treated as friends. So that they feel comfortable and send their friends to visit," he added with a slightly lower voice.

"I have starving children to feed at home," the seller cried out dramatically. I could see the tourist's face twist with pity. Rhanas didn't even bat an eyelid.

"Yeah, most people do at times like these. Drought is never easy to master," he said, unperturbed. "And by the way, I know for example that you, Renésch, are a deceitful little thief. If you really have a wife and children, I retire!"
With these words he turned around and walked towards the shade of the maze of narrow alleyways that surrounded the crowded market place. He heard footsteps behind him. Without

turning around to look at the pathetic features of the tourist, he merged into the mass of people flowing constantly in and out of the market place. The air was heavy from the sweet smell of Geina (a viscous black liquid produced by a variety of cattle, a delicacy in my home town), the loud cries of animals, and the perspiration of hundreds and hundreds of people.

People from Tavura, with their dark skin, mingled with those from Fraxis, with their harsh and sibilant language. Rakourian tribesmen in their white capes, Kasafian slave drivers, proud, veiled women from Ahlia Fevia.
"Hey!" a voice shouted behind Rhanas. "Hey, wait, hey!"

Sighing to himself, he stopped reluctantly and faced him.

"Thanks," he exclaimed, out of breath, his shoulders heaving, "that was a-ma-zing! How you beat down that vendor was absolutely fan-tas-tic!"

Rhanas turned away again and continued walking.
"Hey, wait up!"

I could hear shuffling steps behind me.
"You're a local, right? I mean, obviously with your clothes and your accent when you speak my language and this astonishing, absolutely marvellous deal you just closed for me. But me, I don't really know what to do and I lost my party. Maybe you could help me?"
His eyes were shining from excitement and he looked at me eagerly.

"I have better things to do than to show tourists around. Go to a guide centre!" I said drily. Clearly disappointed the man lowered his head.

"It seemed so artificial to me. They were all polite but they didn't make much effort to help me," he answered.
I hesitated. What was the point? But then I reminded myself of the duty as a host towards a foreign guest and offered him my home as a place to stay until we could find his group.

"So, who are you?" he asked after a while of silently trotting behind me, taking in everything from the colourful clothes of my fellow countrymen to the rich ornaments with which the outer walls of the houses were decorated, even in the poorest areas, to protect from evil Larxons.

Without stopping I answered "Rhanas," and as a sign of good spirit I added "I'm a Guncjan, a healer."

"A Guncjan?" he asked surprised.

"What's wrong with that?" I asked back sharply.

"You don't seem to be somebody I could imagine wanting to help people. Much too emotionally cold if you ask me," he answered, before he could stop himself. He clasped his hands over his mouth and blushed deeply.

Annoyed I sighed and replied, "Do you know me?" and continued walking, pausing from time to time to let the tourist catch up with me after stopping in wonder in front of every little shop.

I felt my thoughts drift to that one day in early autumn, the work designation for all the young men and women aged 17. The lord of this town at that time had proclaimed that the town was in great need of new Guncjans. Nearly half of my year was designated to become healers. Still, if I had the choice, I would choose it again.

Finally we reached the door to my house and working place. I pushed it open and was greeted by the usual heavy smell of herbs, crushed insects and alcohol, for sterilising my instruments, and mixing tinctures and syrups. The long, low room was cramped full with shelves and storage racks. Old books were piled up in the corners. I pulled the curtain open that concealed the staircase leading up to my small flat. "Don't touch anything!" I said, having seen the look on my guest's face, "Some things in here can kill a Harpyn in seconds."

He pulled sharply his hand back from a human skull he was about to touch, with a guilty expression on his face. "I'll have to open the practice in a few minutes, so you might want to go upstairs and rest or have a look round the quarter," I said, suspecting his next question.

"Can't I stay here and watch?" he inquired, as expected.

Weary I shook my head and answered. "No" I said, sitting down "I don't think so. My patients need quiet, *I* need quiet."

But before either of us could say more, the door opened and Madame Xafiare walked in, rushing towards me with her usual expression of constant trouble.

"Oh, Guncjan Rhanas, come quickly, it's my son again and this time I am certain he caught Rhaxuliam. He is all red and stopped breathing and oh, please come quickly!" she cried out.

I sighed to myself, as Madame Xafiare, infamous for her false alarms, fluttered around the shop, accidentally batting the Tarasne herbs, which hung from the low ceiling, with rather more vigour than usual. As always when dealing with the first client of the day, I heaved myself out of the chair unwillingly, but this sounded serious indeed, so I grabbed a bag and quickly filled it with a selection of roots and some Rhaxulanar, a diminutive plant with small white blossoms.

"Please may I come?" the tourist shouted behind us from the stairs as we left the practice. Too impatient to argue I beckoned him to follow and called him a sedan chair, which had to follow the much larger and comfortable palanquin Madame Xafiare owned and both of us used as a means of transport.

When we reached her house and were led through the hallways, an airy quiet hung over the scene.

"Madame," I inquired politely, "where are your servants?"

"Oh," she said, and I could see her blushing through the semidarkness, "they are all on their day off."

"All at once?" I dug deeper.

"Oh, oh yes. It is, err, a special day today for servants," she answered without looking at me.

"A special day off? Mm, haven't heard anything about such a day, but well, if you say so Madame," I said politely. The tourist looked at me questioningly but I only shook my head.

"What is this Rhaxuliam?" he asked after a while of following us through the grand rooms with only the tapping of our feet against the marble floor to disturb the silence.

"It's a virus which enters through the airways and peculiarly through the skin as well. It is spread via Rhaxuls, which..."

"What is a Rhaxul?" he interrupted me. I sighed to myself before answering.

"A Rhaxul is a butterfly-like animal. Its right wing is speckled and its left wing is striped. The powder from its wings carries the virus which uses the Rhaxul as a host. They are quite common and wherever they land, fly, touch...they leave this powder which can lead to..."

"...to red spots across the skin which swell rapidly, it infects the throat and causes breathing problems. Basically strong allergic reactions," Madame Xafiare completed. I inclined my head towards her approvingly.

"Aha, and how do you treat it?" the tourist continues asking.

" By a mixture of squashed roots with leaves of the Rhaxulanar, the plant you've seen in my practice."

Finally we reached the door of the room where the sick boy was supposed to be and I handed out protective masks to Madame Xafiare and the tourist before putting mine on as a precaution against the virus.
"Are you sure you want to see this?" I asked the tourist, who nodded with tightly closed lips before pulling the mask with sweet herbs over his nose and mouth. I pushed open the door and entered.

What I found was contrary to all my expectations. The little boy lay in his bed, his eyes close, no sign of swollen red dots or shortness of breath, but his face was shining with sweat, his skin looked furrowed from all the water loss, I could see the traces where somebody had tried to wipe off the blood mingled with tear fluid from under his eyes. From his mouth more blood trickled onto his chest. He looked as pale as Death herself, and I could see his small chest straining to get the last breath he might have left on this side. I knew immediately that this was not something you encountered and walked away alive. This was Shinatos, Instant Death, capable of killing a person in under an hour. The tourist shrank back against the wall and the Madame shrieked loudly.
"Oh my darling, oh my love! What happened to you?"

"You knew this," I said coldly. "You knew it wasn't a normal allergic reaction."

"He didn't look like that when I left him," she cried out and flung herself over her son's body.

"When did you leave him?" I asked roughly pulling her away from the boy.

"Half an hour ago," she sobbed "when he suddenly started to sweat so much."

"I need hot water, now!" I ordered her sharply, as a trace of haughtiness flickered over her face and changed quickly back to sobbing. She ran to get the water.

I opened my pouch and quickly scanned the contents. I had taken some Lezruw as I was planning to add it to the Rhaxulanar to heal the non-existent, allergic reaction. It was a very rare and expensive, thorny herb and the only thing I knew that might cure the Instant Death. I felt my face tensing as I was calculating how much I needed for the little boy, Madame Xafiare, the tourist and myself. I estimated that the Madame might still have four servants left in the house – a cook, a butler and two house maids, hidden somewhere. It should be enough for everyone. The Madame came back a short while later with two kettles. I ordered the tourist to try to give some warm water to the boy to replace the water he had lost and added the Lezruw and some pulverised mushrooms to the boiling hot water in the second kettle. Then I turned to the woman.
"Now, the truth! Where are your servants, Madame?" I asked fiercely because I feared the worst.

She didn't answer at once but shied away from me. I grabbed her arm.
"The truth, now! It might not be too late yet."

"In the cellar, I had to lock them away, didn't I?" she murmured finally.

"The key!" I said, stretching out my hand. Reluctantly she handed it over. I ran out of the room looking for the wooden staircase leading down to Madame Xafiare's cellar. Quickly I opened the door and found a low room cramped with shelves, full of jars containing pickled and dried fruits, geina, large sacks full of flour for bread- making, vegetables in all forms and shapes, eggs, bottles filled with the exquisite yellow-green of a first-class wine and …… people. A cook, a butler – and three house maids, easily recognisable by their uniforms, squinted at the light coming from the cellar's entrance. I could feel an uneasy tingle mixing with my tension. It might be enough, I told myself, it might just work out.

The cook and one of the maids already bore the first marks of the Instant Death – a sweaty, feverish expression and terrible weakness. Both were either sitting or lying down. There was a grim tenseness in the air, they knew why their mistress had locked them away by now – to prevent them from going to the local authorities and reporting the case of the sick boy, with the effect that the whole house would have had to be locked up, the inhabitants left to die if no help from a Guncjan reached them in time.

The Shinatos was too dangerous to risk the spreading of the disease by letting potentially ill people into contact with others. "Come upstairs!" I said "And bring the sick!"

Then I left. When I re-entered the room where the ill boy lay I was pleased to notice that the brew had finished brewing. I poured some down his throat, taking care of him only taking small sips. Then I let all the servants, Madame Xafiare and the tourist drink one mouthful, as a cure and a precaution. In the end nothing was left, and I had no more Lezruw.

The tingle grew into a twitch, but I calmed myself down by reminding myself that in my practice at home I had some more stored herb. But a slight feeling of uneasiness pinched my heart and remained. Over the next ten minutes I watched the boy's face relax and saw his breathing stabilise. Shortly I took leave of Madame Xafiare and the gratitude of her servants and made my way home. A slight doubt came into m mind that I might be contaminated myself, and that I would put many people in danger by leaving the house. But I felt as if I had no choice and if it would be me or them it would be me. The feeling of uneasiness grew stronger with every step I took and coming nearer my home, I could feel my breath getting shallower and faster, but I blamed that on the excitement of the past hour. Shinatos is not an easy opponent. And I'd have to send a report to the local representation of the government.

I flung open my door and hastened to one of the shelf in the furthest corner, opening one jar after the other. Nothing – all empty. When I had opened the last flagon my courage fell. Nothing left in my house. Suddenly I heard a loud clank.

"What's wrong?" the tourist asked nervously as I stared down on the broken shards of the flagon which had slid through my sweaty fingers. For a moment everything went black and I had to lean against the wall for support.
"What's wrong?" the tourist asked again, with increasingly alarm.

"What do you think?" I gasped with effort.

"You knew this would happen?" the tourist, said in shock.
"I...miscalculated the amount," I groaned through clenched teeth. Liar, a small voice said in my head.
The tourist looked on helplessly as I slowly slid down the bleached out wall and started doubling over, coughing up blood.
"My ..... pouch!" I panted and tried to stay conscious until the tourist had brought me the desired object.

"Open... it" I ordered hoarsely and with a horrible effort I feverishly groped for the herb I had used to heal the little boy and his family, but even before my fingers touched the little compartment in the bag I normally used to store it in I knew it was hopeless. The last crumbling leaves had been given to the tourist to save his life. Maybe he had known that these were the last Lezruws leaves available in this town before he gave the brew to the tubby man kneeling next to him and shouting for help. Just before he slipped into nothingness he gathered his last strength and patted the man on the shoulder. He could feel Death watching him, like a mother waiting for a long gone child to return. His hand fell down and his soul followed his gaze up through the window to the sky.

The Punishment for Stealing

This is the official test and punishment for stealing, from the Book of Trials and Punishments, recognised by the Royal Judiciary of Iole Sinistra.

A person suspected of stealing, and so accused by no fewer than two witnesses over the age of 12 and not being under the influence of spirit from within or without, shall be placed in a pit with an unfed Truggle[1].

The person so accused and placed in the pit shall be required to sing to the Truggle until it either falls asleep, which indicates innocence, or until the Truggle attacks. The creature is particularly sensitive to the tone of the singer, and is instinctively enraged by shaky, nervous singing or tones of guilt carried by a singing voice.

A Truggle's attack generally leaves the guilty party without fingers, which is the punishment for stealing.

Truggles should not be used for song trials past the age of about four, when they become too bad-tempered to make the trial a fair one, and when they become strong enough to bite off whole limbs.

---

[1] a small, cat-sized carnivore found only in the foothills of the Red Mountains

Author's note of interest:

It is still illegal in Iole to have singing lessons. However, singing teachers are highly sought after by criminal gangs, especially in the major cities. The illegal black market in singing lessons is controlled by the secretive Piccoli Caste, a 'mafia' of castrati, operating from sound-proofed underground chambers. These vice rings are notoriously difficult to infiltrate and hence to uncover, due to their custom of wearing shirts and long socks, but absolutely nothing in between. The best way to shut down an illegal singing lesson is to send in a pack of young truggles. Anything resembling a finger is likely to be bitten clean off.

People of The Sands

The ancient tale of Beodor is presented for the first time in translation from the Curamic Language of the Desert People.

Between rustic tents and thick layers of dusty sand awakes Beodor. Bone-breaking daily labour has taken its toll on his trained and conditioned body; he must rise nonetheless, the tribe's survival rests in each and every pair of hands and feet they can procure.

Beodor stretches his muscular arms towards the balmy light illuminating the inside of the tent. He steps outside, studying the all-familiar sight of the infinite orange sands wherever his gaze wanders. Already he is thinking of the task that lies ahead; he must navigate the group that gathers the holy element, three suns from their current location in the direction of helia*. Beodor knows that he must leave soon, as many have disgracefully fallen to the lethal rays of Mother Light. She is very austere when it comes to the times when we mortals may bathe in her holy light. The ones that are recalcitrant die, we are not permitted to speak or think of them any longer.

A small group of Beodor's fellow Waterers wave at him fervently from afar. Their skin, charcoal black, stands in crass contrast to their milky white letter tunics, with their feet wrapped in the surplus leather of the clothing fabricants. Cooked up to unbearable temperatures in the course of the day, the orange sand is excruciating to the bare foot and impossible to be crossed without protection. Beodor is constantly reminded of the danger of the sands through the blessing that befell him one day. He was marching obliviously, when suddenly his right foot was interrupted mid-stride by a pointed rock, piercing through the upper layer of sand. He could not possibly catch his fall so he stretched his hands to minimize the exposure to the searing ground... no man could possible endure the heat. Beodor instantly, through a detrimental reflex, retreated his beaming red hands, writhing in horrific pain. He lost his balance once more, saw his tunic engulfed in thick, black smoke, and feinted. Most of his body is now covered in chalk-white, intricately intertwining ornaments of the most beautiful scar tissue. A sign of fierce strength and sacred wisdom, whoever truthfully attains them is treated with reverence, who is found guilty for intentionally inflicting wounds to oneself must face intense repercussions, enforced by the Hunters of the tribe.

Beodor grabs for his white tunic without wasting a glance back, trotting blithely to the other Waterers. The group comprises three of his brothers and two of his uncles. They all look at Beodor's scarred face approvingly.

"Good morning, Stone-Seer* Beodor, Mother Light smiles on you."

The Waterers speak with varied intonation, albeit all with composed admiration, as he joins the round.

"Good morning, Carrier Pent, Carrier Gra, Carrier Lero, good morning to ye too, Hunter Rado and Healer Unuti, Mother Light cries for you," announces Beodor, deep affection flooding his heart as he looks from face to face of these proud men. "We must now depart again, to find the holy element and harvest it, and return it to our people once more!"

And thus begins their journey, leading them through steep sand valleys and countless orange dunes. The sun burns down on their backs belligerently.

"Can you see the Helia stone, my fellow companions? It shall not be long now," utters Beodor through clenched teeth, little rivers of sweat meandering down his broad forehead.

"Stone-Seer, Mother Light is angry, no? Why does she make such heat come from the sky?" carrier Pent inquires of him.

"I cannot speak to her holiness like Rashi Oran, our omniscient father may, though I may speak with confidence when I say that her powers of the day are good, as they are evil during the night."

"Yes, may the light meet your words, Beodor!" mumbles Healer Unuti, "we must be undivided in our deeds, or we shall perish."

"Ready your baskets, Waterers, we have arrived!" Beodor points at the crystal clear fluid that is suddenly revealed as they reach the edge of a giant water basin, "Is it not wonderful, my friends, let us thank Mother Light for her indulgence."

Each one of them voices their gratitude as they scoop the clear fluid into their bowls. The total of the load they now carry will last the tribe for an entire day. If they do not return, a few must die of thirst. Such is the harsh reality of their arid environment. And thus these men walk with their chins raised high and their spirits lifted, defying the great heat of the desert and the back-breaking poundage they now shoulder. But something is different today. At first they are all perfectly unaware of the signs: a searing heat, unusual even for the capricious climate of the orange sands. For Mother Light, the god of these simple people, has already forsaken them by changing her emission spectrum into a lethal dose.

"I am weak. What I do wrong?" cried Carrier Gra.

"I feel it too, brother, do not worry, think of your wife and child," reassured Beodor.

"I cannot, it hurts… too…" and Gra starts tipping over, his eyes rolling upwards.

Reflexively Healer Unuti throws the water basket on her head, and with great prowess she catches the Carrier whilst keeping basket and body in equilibrium.

With a grave expression on his face, and a wet-eyed glance thrown towards all the remaining men, Healer Unuti reveals,"He cannot carry on, I may have a remedy, but look! it is a disaster, the light! We have no time, I fear, we must leave him behind."

And as men of duty, they trust the most educated man of the group on the matter. No one departs without a brief blessing and a word of love for their friend, but then the matter is settled, and they must continue. But one after another the men fall obscurely to a terrible, invisible foe that is devouring life after life without mercy, never granting their dearest possession to these modest men: honor.

Only Beodor and Unuti remain. Their life energy is rapidly fading, with sunken, delirious eyes they scan the horizon for signs of their village, hopelessly lost on an endless field of barren land. They have decided to carry two baskets each, one on their head and one on their aching arms.

"I must. I must. Sarania! Oh, my pregnant woman!" thinks Beodor.

"All those men. Bah! Do not be a fool, old man, more can be saved by leaving them behind..." Unuti suddenly sinks onto the orange ground, lifeless like an oversized doll. The water spills, hissing like a ferocious snake as it evaporates. Beodor screams in agony.

"What is this hellish curse! " But Beodor is not bitter, not despairing yet. It takes his remaining mental strength to resuscitate his powerful faith, "Mother Light, I am your servant. If this is what I deserve, I will take it without any pity. I need no explanation, I need no sign. I trust in you, I trust in you..."

Glossary:

Helia: One of the five directions of the "People of the Sands". Their navigation system is based on the original five stones (helia, reyna, uhuna, ashati, trulam) located in their primary settlement. They have a serious of other locations where they have placed these stones, but a skilled Stone-Seer had to trace the route there first.

Stone-Seer: A person endowed with the ability of walking into a particular direction for an extensive period of time without deviation.

The Legend of Teg

High up and away in the Yutway Range of Eastern Iole, far beyond where town has given way to village, village to hamlet, and hamlet to farmstead, and where farmstead reluctantly steps aside for woodsman's lodge, sprawls the Forest of Jaggery. It cloaks the hills in orange, except in Autumn, when bark turns to purple, then to black when the yellow hoare-frost and the blue snows come. At this height, basking in the full force of midnight's ionizing radiation, no over-large, soft-bodied animals survive. The spiny murtz, the armoured peckle, the flying shurlock and the sabersnutch, which buries itself as the sun turns purple at each day's end, are each no larger than a doglick, tough and largely herbivorous, except in the depth of winter. Smaller, furry creatures, scuttle up and down the rubbery trunks of the trees, living both on them and within them. They are the Mafgherli, and each night they climb to the highest branches to face the full force of the toxic radiation. Each night they absorb and change, greeting the warmth of the red dawn as new genetic forms, their bodies changeable as clay, as resilient as hammered lead. They eat the trees, they eat the animals of the forest and they feed on each another as each day the food web restructures itself and animals find their niches anew. Men avoid them; their flesh is too toxic for humans to eat, their fur too allergenic to wear against bare skin. The Mafgherli fear humans, just as they fear each other, and generally keep their distance....but then again, in the Forest of Jaggery every rule that can be written can also be broken between red-up and sun-blue, as the sun cycles on; a great stationary eye. It is the size of a fist at arm's reach, pouring its energy into the waiting creatures below, glowing with a father's pride. Perhaps it is a little sad that it cannot watch its children grow and change, that it knows not what they become or how they act out their existence in its radiant field. And, above all, it knows not its own strength.

The red-up was greeted with such beautiful song that it appeared the day could only bring good things. First impressions are not always reliable. Teg's window was thrown wide open to let in the warmth, and this always made her sing her head off. When in such a mood she became a veritable pluterdrink. There was no-one to match her in the mountains, for her gift was great, even more than she or her family could have known.

'Ow! Ow!' came the chorus of approval from outside, where Loty was fetching melt-water from the brook, and digging some curleybups for soup. 'Sing 'Oh Merhwen, my Okky'! You sing it well enough for the Soferex himself. If he ever hears of you, we'll none of us be spared, but brought to court in the Dreadful Smoke. Oh,

Merhwen, My Okky, A finger-bred fool are you, to have wandered so far, to have challenged the Ghwar....'

Loty stopped himself singing, as Teg took up the tune, her voice smoothly reaching up and down the scale. She had the voice of an angel-dream, the balm of a heated milk-sop, babbling over bathstones.

'Teg! Come and get your breakfast!' her mother called from the kitchen. The smell of frizzled slingops was drifting through the house. The radiation shutters were all slung wide open just after red-up each day, and the business of gathering food and making music would begin. It was a tradition of the woodland families to make music whenever they worked. In the long evenings, when they shut themselves up inside the house, everyone played an instrument or two, and everyone would sing. At her stove, Teg's mother took up the chorus of 'Oh Merhwen', harmonising and encouraging Loty to rejoin them in his rich baritone, not bad for a twelve year-old. Sniddy was only five, and Gvonly eight, but they were both capable of holding their part in the family choir, Gvonly's voice was starting to break nicely, his mother noticed. He would entertain them for many an evening in the future, whilst the house was gated against the burning radiation of the evening and night, and outside of this safe zone the creatures of the forest either hid or basked in the daily radiant storm.

'Where's Father?' asked Gvonly, helping himself to a muffin.

'He went to check the edge of the forest. You know how people have been talking about encroachment. He is taking some measurements each day.'

'Is it true?' he asked. 'Have the trees learnt how to move?'

'Will the forest eat us up? Will our house be safe, Mama?' asked Sniddy, sounding not in the least concerned, as she took a plate of fringops, sliced and oiled them, and over-dusted them with ogg powder.

'Course not,' said Gvonly, 'No way. The trees may puff up and explode if you don't pay them attention, but they never move far away from the rock and the hard waters of the cave system. I learnt it at school.'

Once every month, there was a session for the children, held in Gerthuia, a four hour walk over the rocky outcrops known locally as Ghett Cleff. The gatherers and woods-families of the area took their children along to the 'school' and between them offered classes in geography, biology, music, art, and anything else of practical interest. Next year, Sniddy would travel there for the first time. What a great time they always had, all camping overnight in special, safe tents, eating and drinking with the other families, swapping stories and, above all, singing songs and making music. What a shame that poor Teg had never been able to go. She had always been left at home at these times, with her mother when younger, but now she was older she stayed with Sniddy and they sang songs whilst the family was away. When Sniddy went to school for the first time, then Teg would also be alone for the first time. Nothing could be done. Teg was always last into breakfast, too, and for the same reason that she could never manage the perilous passage of Ghett Cleff: she was blind.

Teg had been born that way, unlike many of the blind folk of the forest, whose error had been to stay out too late, as the sun's radiant energy cycled towards the ultra-violet. Their eyes had been burned and scarred by looking to the sky at the wrong time. Teg had never known the shifting colours of the sky and forest, but with the absence of sight, her hearing had become her dominant sense. She knew just where she was in the house by the dampening of her voice, and she was able to walk by herself all the way to the forest edge, which involved crossing Smoke Bridge and wading across the Fortune Stream at times of year when it was just passable. She followed the sounds of nature.

One spring, resting on the bridge, she thought she heard a meadow wafkin sing. This rare visitor to the high mountains sang with a long, throaty warble. Teg listened so intently to this new sound that she began to hear words form inside her head, 'Sing for me, Teg! The old, fading souls need to hear a fresh voiced girl. Sing for your elders! Sing for your keepers! Even here, as we are, we hear your clear voice, so perfect.'

Teg thought to herself that the voice had come from the upper levels, and smiled secretly that some poor soul, trapped there and fading to white, had been listening to her song and had thought to send the wafkin to thank her. The old magic of the upper levels had been a fabulous and exciting part of her grandmother's tales. The heroes and heroines of her stories had left their Miraban flesh and blood bodies behind, risking lives to send their tethered souls to the higher planes, for glory, for salvation, perhaps to achieve some victory in the Yutanga War, which pitched the pale skinned lowlanders against the blue-black clans of the Yutway.

Teg's own skin was more blue than black, taking after her grandmother in so many ways. Her sightless eyes of evening violet were flecked with the orange of morning as if a painter intent on loading his brush with the colours of the morn had flicked the paint right into them.

The part of the day when cares were at their most free was about to pass, and a noulder-rick was about to fly across the sun, bringing winter's bitter chill to late spring promise. Loty brought the bad news in the front door.
'Come, quick, Mother! It's Father...he's hurt.'

The young man of fourteen long-cycles bounded back out into the brilliance of morning, where Father was lying on the pale yellow grass, blue bees pollinating the luterflowers around his legs. A black stain of blood was soaking his coarse fabric trousers and his breathing was shallow and rapid. Mother and Loty were followed quickly to his aid by Gvonly, whilst Sniddy hugged up to Teg, who listened, her violet eyes darting around in thought.
'Oaargh, Dallimurgh, Father, what has happened to you?'

Mother carefully started to roll up what was left of his left trouser leg. There was clotted blood and pieces of ragged, torn cloth in the wound. He winced and made a sound between gritted teeth when she finally found his shattered leg with gentle fingers. What a mess. He had lost blood and there could be infection. He may need to stay out after sun-blue tonight, to cauterise and sterilise this wound.
'What happened, Dalli? Did you get your leg caught in a crevice. Those rocks are so dangerous, you shouldn't have been climbing the ridge alone!' she said, as gently as she could.

'No, Potomah, this is not an accident. I was attacked by Mafgherli, a dozen or more. I have never seen such aggression from them. I did not think it possible.'

'The woodsman Ulljhoch was missing last week. He has not returned to his family on Windy Cleush,' said Loty. 'Do you think they have mutated? Have they taken savage, like they did two summers ago. You know, they killed a yutboar which was tied to a fence, well away from the forest. Was it like that?'

'No, Loty. I don't think it was like that. They are clever now, working together, they never did this, not with human, never before,' he said, weakly.

'Come, get him into the house! Get this wound washed and let him rest!' Mother glanced once back towards the woods as she said this, as if she feared that her husband had been followed. There was nothing there to see. The forest was brilliant white now, and any Mafgherli would be resting in the shade, waiting for sun-blue.

The family gathered around Dallimurgh's bed, bringing steaming water from the deep, hot well and fresh soup made with crushed fringops and aesies. Teg took her father's hand. 'Are we safe, Father, is the forest changing again?'

Every few years there were major changes in the forest which could have profound effects on the lives of the woodsmen and gatherers. Could this be the start of one of these difficult transitions? He opened his eyes and looked up at Teg's sightless, but fine-featured expression. It was a pretty face, burnished black with blue high-lit cheek bones, drawn by concern.

Instead of replying to her question, he tried to sit up and called for Mah and Loty. 'You need to fetch the other families, and get word to Gerthuia.'

'No, Dalli, what can have caused such a thing to be necessary? Are you sure we must do this?' his wife implored, seeing that her husband had lost blood, and was perhaps light-headed and subject to daytime dreaming.

'Mah, Loty, listen to me! They came at me from the trees. They were working together, as one. I defended myself with my nefter, and parted several Mafgherli heads from their bodies, but they were so quick. My mistake was to enter the shade of the trees. It has been so long since there has been any trouble…but this is different. They were strong, and not afraid. I got away by chance of the hour, red-up was already under way and they were loath to follow me out of the deep shade. I ran for my life, beloved; or they would have killed me I am sure. Make sure the others know! And tell them that… the forest is on the move. There were trees around Djain's Pond and all the way along the lower ravine, as far as First Rock.'

With that final effort, Father lay back and closed his eyes. He was too weak to give them any more. The forest was moving? Could the stories be true, then? And what of this new face of the Mafgherli? As they bustled around the house, seeing to their injured father, preparing themselves for a dangerous journey in the afternoon, with time against them, Teg held Sniddy close to her and started to sing. Her song was a soothing one, a lullaby from the old days, and soon Sniddy was humming along, her troubles placed on the wayside, and her father was sleeping a healing sleep, his dark features, just beginning the peel of middle age, a mask of peace.

There was literally no time to lose; food was thrown into way-packs, and water into snerkins for the trek. It could just be done, there and back to the Cleush, taking the longer route that ran away from the forest and followed the river. Once there, they could stay overnight, and Loty could be sent on to Gerthuia alone or with one of the Hjirett daughters. Piurty Hjirett was fifteen and strong enough to make such a journey in a day.

Mother wanted to get back to the house by sun-blue the same day. She did not want to leave little Sniddy and Gvonly alone with her blind daughter overnight. Not when there was such danger on the doorstep and her husband was sick. There was no knowing how the poison in the Mafgherli's bite might have mutated too, and whether his life would yet be taken by the attack in the forest.
'Bye, my darlings,' she said, hugging them close and tight. 'If we don't return by sun-blue, you know what to do?' She didn't need to say more.

They knew how and when the house must be shuttered and all kept inside. 'If Father takes worse, give him drops of blue-bee nectar from the larder jars, heated with little powfett. Don't leave him outside unless…unless you have to, and then only for a short while after sun-blue…and cover yourselves!' She added.

The children nodded in silence and returned her hugs more strongly. There were times when the young had to listen in silence and be strong, and this was one of them. In this mood of resilience and defiance, Teg thought again of the tales her grandmother had told. Perhaps, what they needed was one of the heroes of her stories to send his soul to the higher planes and to put things right on Miraba, just like the stories she had told them again and again. But even if the old stories were partly true, nobody remembered how to do this for real. Only special people, born different from the rest, were able to disconnect the soul from flesh and ascend a slender tether to the higher planes. When this was done, the body would collapse, as if dead. If the hero could successfully navigate through the mists of the in-between levels, even then there would be the challenge of performing the rituals that meant so little on the higher planes, but changed so much on the human plane of Miraba. 'Years in the training,' said her grandmother, 'people spent just minutes in order to perform some miracle or great work'. Teg often thought of them, and wondered, and wished. There were also stories of disaster, of course, of accidents and of souls trapped for eternity until they started to fade. She thought of the wafkin and wondered about what she thought she had heard on the bridge.

Sniddy went outside to see her mother and elder brother disappear over the scrub and out into the whitening mist. They turned to wave twice, and it was almost as if they were off on a summer picnic. At this time of day it was generally too bright to see the edge of the forest, but Sniddy still gave a fearful glance in its direction, cupping her face in her hands in order to see better. There was nothing to see except for meadows, shrinking into the distance, giving way to a white line where the sky met the forest in the glare of the midday sun. Gvonly watched from the window, his eyes glazed and unfocused, a little bored already. He watched a grossel slither along the drainage channel from the house and disappear into the long grass, and wished he was allowed to do something useful to help. He wanted to slide away from the house too, down to the forest. He could take a gatterbolt with him and some slugs, and bag a few Mafgherli before his mother returned; get in a little bit of instant revenge for the attack on his father. He had been to the forest many, many times. He knew the way; there was nothing to be afraid of.

He had hunted shurlocks several times, alongside his brother, as his father had unsettled them from their brood-shelves on the edge of the forest, with his great horn. Gvonly was a better shot than his brother, for his age, and his father had often called him, "Little Gvonly, the great hunter of Jaggery, who brings the food to table," to which his son had always puffed up his chest and walked a little taller.'

As Sniddy went back inside, Gvonly had already gone to find his gatterbolt and his hunting hat.

Potomah and Loty walked quickly and quietly, breaking their silence from time to time with small talk. They wondered 'How tall had Piurty grown since they had last seen her?' and 'Would there still be any patches of snow up on the Midlock at this time of year?'

They were thirsty and tired by the time they reached the homestead, and the sun was very green indeed. They would generally have been outside now, enjoying the time with some gardening or some light repairment. This was also a good time for a game of frab-ball in the field. Loty would form a team with Sniddy against their father and Gvonly, with Mother watching from the window and Teg listening and smiling at the sounds of them fighting over the ball. There would be cups of muswick tea with slices of apple, as the green deepened and the temperature dropped. This was a fertile place, with food a-plenty for those skilled in hunting and gathering, and plenty of time left to kick back and enjoy life.

 Sometimes the rain drove them inside, particularly if the summer was late-end, and they would play cards instead, with the windows fully open to the sound of rain outside. Teg would be able to play cards with a partner, and Loty was particularly helpful and patient in whispering the name of each card into her ear and repeating it again whenever she forgot.

The Hjirett house was higher up in altitude than even their own. It was protected from the northern gales by a rocky outcrop, and had a commanding view of the forest below. Any fires or drought zones could be seen from this viewpoint, and the Hjiretts had, by all accounts, one of the best spots. At this altitude it was even more urgent to get inside by sun-blue, as the radiation was even stronger than below, and a person's skin could easily be burnt right off their face by just a few minute's exposure. This was even true of the blue-blackest of the locals, let alone the pale skinned travellers who strayed this far from the cities of the plane, looking for adventure. As for the midnight sun, well no-one had lived to tell of the effects of this. The occasional traveller had been found, bones whitened and still smoking, but not a word to say of what had befallen. The Hjirett's shutters were double thickness, and their roof was replaced each year with fresh rock slices and re-daubed with ant-grease to block out the midnight menace.

At last they turned the path around the steep rock wall to get their first view of the house. Mother called out 'Hello! Good Meet, This Greening!' several times, so as not to catch the family unawares, but without response.

There were two very inauspicious signs, as they rounded the shelf. The first was that there were trees where none should have been. The forest normally ended a good half hiothetre as the mercury flowed, but today it seemed to be lapping right up to the rocks below the house. There were scattered trees, even in the garden of the house, and they leaned threateningly. Soon, they saw why their calls would not be answered, and why they needed to turn back now.
'Oh, Mother, look at the roof!' gasped Loty, drawing a short nefter from its sheath.

Potomah was a strong, fair and athletic woman of forty long-cycles. She was a few cycles younger than her husband, and a good trekker, huntress and forager. She also made the best brunch-egg waffles in the Yutway. She was blond, with blue skin, whilst her son was darker and more like her husband. She had made many journeys and seen many strange things in both forest and mountain, but nothing more unusual or more frightening than this. The house of Hjirett was in ruins, one tree having punched a hole in the roof, and two of its henchmen standing as if shaking the walls to pieces. The windows were shattered and the roof had collapsed with one of the walls. You could see into the rooms, where the furniture stood; nothing seemed to be moved or taken.

This was a lived-in house, suddenly taken by force, and there was no sign of the occupants.

They moved a little closer, and noticed that the front door was open, and hanging by a twisted hinge, as if a giant had ripped it from its seating.

'Easy, Loty…best not go straight in!' she cautioned her son, placing one hand on his shoulder, and drawing a blade in her other. 'May the Soferex save us! Let's just look from the outside.'

They cautiously walked around the front of the house, glancing down the cliff to where trees seemed to be intent on climbing, gnarled hand over claw, to reach them. If the trees moved, there was no evidence of that right now. They were frozen in the act and, if they were still moving, it was not whilst being watched, or else it was slow like the hour hand of a clock. They peered in, nervously, and even shouted once or twice to attract the attention of anyone left inside. There was a pot of tea on the table, and a plate of crumbs charred black. There were chairs overturned and the legs of a bed stuck down through the ceiling from one of the bedrooms. This damage looked recent, but perhaps some days old. There could be no-one here. Not alive. With the shutters open and the roof breached, the house would be sterile of life by now. Nevertheless, something moved. Loty was sure that something had moved in the deep blue-green shadow and then out of sight behind a chunk of fallen roofing.

'We need to get back,' said Mother, thinking that she, too, had seen something move at the edge of her vision.

'I want to go home,' said Loty, his nefter raised and shaking slightly.

'Back down the path, quickly!' said Potomah, her blond plait swinging with her head as she looked from side to side, in rising panic.

The first Mafgherli to hit them jumped from the guttering and landed on Loty's head. He threw it off in fear and fury, shouting, before it could dig in its claws, and it scampered away to the shadows. As Potomah turned to see this, another one struck her on the ankle and bit deep and painfully, whilst another hit her in the stomach, causing her to double up. She flung this one away from her and hacked down on the furry body attached to her foot, as two more came in from behind, one scrabbling up and over her back and the other biting into the back of her knee, making her sag and sink to the ground. Its saliva burnt horribly, as it touched the wound, and started its journey towards the heart. Locals had some immunity, and this would rarely cause death.

Loty was over in a flash to rescue his mother. He dragged one of the things away from her neck and it gave him a nip in the process, which felt like a hot flame. Then he prised the other one from her leg and flung it away. If there were more to come, he was taking no chances. He stood in front of her, waving the machete around, ready for anything that might come his way, from any angle.

Potomah quickly stood, although shaken and bleeding, there was no serious damage yet, and then they ran, as fast as they could, back along the path and away from the house. They ran without looking back, without thinking.

They ran until their lungs were bursting and they were out of sight and out of reach of that terrifying building, and away from the trees, back by the river where they could wash the blood away from their various bites, cool the stinging of the poison, and splash their faces with cold water. They were an hour from sun-blue, and there was no time to discuss what had happened. They had to get home, and fast!

At just before sun-blue, Sniddy started to close up the house. She stood on tables and chairs, wherever they were well placed, in order to reach up and close shutters.

'Gvonly!' she shouted, several times, 'Where are you? Please come and help!'

Her brother was that much taller and stronger than her, he would get the house shut up properly in half the time. This was typical of Gvonly, to go missing when there was work to be done. If only Teg could help, she would be twice as much use as her brother, even on a good day.

Teg was helping in any way she could. She slowly made her way around the bedrooms, closing shutters and, each time, listening with her head slightly cocked to the sounds of the outdoors. She could hear the distant cry of a rishemew, as it hunted far above the ridge, hanging in the thin air on paper wings. The stream was singing, as it always did, slightly quieter than usual for lack of recent rain. The bees were zinging around the meadow, noisily sucking nectar, and field mice and crockets were going about their business, each with their own signature of sound that only Teg could hear. The one sound that seemed out of place was a distant one, on the verge even of Teg's supreme sensitivity. She thought for a moment that she could hear the rustling of leaves, the deep-throated murmur of the trunks, the creaking of branches. Was that the sound of the Mafgherli, the shadow creatures speaking in their strange, outlandish voices, half in the human spectrum of hearing, and half in the ultrasonic frequencies?

She could smell the dampness and spicy tones of the old, decaying bark and drooling resin, as if the forest was at the foot of the garden, and not almost two hiothetres across the scrub. Puzzled, she closed the bedroom shutters and bolted them, shutting out the strange sounds and smells. Father was still sleeping, the afternoon was now deep blue, and she had instructions to follow and smaller children to look after. Teg could hear Sniddy singing as she shut up the kitchen, but of Gvonly there was still no sound. She began to sing along with her little sister, picking up her tempo with a 'Hey-diddle-hey, a bread and a bardle, to-day, to-day!', when there was a scream and a number of plates and cups crashed to the ground and shattered. It was Sniddy, from the kitchen, shouting, and a terrible noise of bashing, as if pots and pans were being used like hammers. As fast as she could, but with consternation, she felt her way to the stairs and down towards the commotion.

'What is it, Sniddy? What's the matter? Wait there, I'm coming!' she shouted.

The sounds of battle had subsided by the time she arrived, and Sniddy was sitting with her back to the range, sobbing and panting heavily.

'Oh, Teg! I think I've killed it,' she managed to say, between sobs.

Teg could not see what it was, of course, but she could certainly smell its smoked-rubber fur and she guessed correctly that the creature Sniddy had referred to was Mafgherli. She trod on a saucepan lid and slipped clumsily, whilst trying to find her little sister, and almost fell on her, where she sat on the kitchen floor. She gave Sniddy a comforting cuddle as soon as she could find her with her arms outstretched.

'Where is it, my dear fulsop? What happened?'

'It jumped down from above just as I was taking a last look outside the door for Gvonly. It got caught up in my hair, and I bashed it off. I hit it with anything I could find.'

'Gvonly!' gasped Teg, to herself and her sister, 'What is he doing outside after blue? The silly boy!' Her hand brushed against the body of the Mafgherli, and she immediately felt the itchiness of its fur on the back of her hand. She brought her hand back to it, without thinking, and allowed her palm to span its chest. She listened and waited for a moment, whilst Sniddy looked on.

'It isn't dead, my fulsop, just stunned…and perhaps also injured. It breathes slowly but its heart still skips along.'

'Should we finish it?' asked the little girl, with distaste.

'No,' Teg replied, thoughtfully and with surprising tenderness, 'but neither can we put it outside, it is past sun-blue, and we must keep our doors and windows bolted tonight, unless Gvonly returns.' She paused. 'I expect he followed Mah and Loty up to the Hjirett's. He'll be there, safe in the house now, I expect, singing some of the forest songs they so love up on the Ridge. He'll be drinking muswick tea by the fire.'

She started to sing one of the forest songs, her voice stretching up by arpeggio, bringing to mind the highest feathered tops, and then softly sinking into minor key, like the dying of the light in the deep forest. Teg's eyes were distant as she sang, and when she finished there were tears running down her nose, which she was careful not to drip on her sister snuggled into her, unaware of her pain. The strange creature lying on the floor was now sleeping rather than unconscious, its hurt and anger taken away by the beauty and poignancy of the song of the forest. Teg, however, cried for her brother, whom she feared she would never see again in this world.

Potomah smeared great, thick handfuls of ant grease over Loty's face and arms, from the emergency kit that all Yuitians carried as a matter of course. Anyone caught outside in the deep-blue would need to cover all exposed skin against the harsh ultraviolet of the evening sun. Loty had only been out at this time for a few minutes before, so the touch and smell of ant grease was unfamiliar, and a little unpleasant. They also had to put on very odd-looking wooden eye shades, with thin slits, through which the way ahead could be viewed in a limited way. Carefully shaped overhangs, at brow level, would protect their sensitive corneas from exposure and damage.

Even with precautions, they had to move as fast as they could, as the later the evening became, the harsher the ultraviolet, until it would penetrate thin cloth, then even thick fabric or leather, and after that...only the bleached skeletons sometimes found in the woods knew the final outcome. Few creatures, such as the Mafgherli (curse them for their mutant habits) could survive and even thrive in this environment. Even the leaves of the trees curled up and branches hung limply, shying away from the treacherous midnight rays, as the sun cycled through the spectrum and finally back to infrared, when the ground was once again warmed lovingly, and shutters could be thrown open at red-up.

Loty had never seen the ultra flowers snap open their highly patterned forms, nor the buzz-moths appear in sudden clouds, summoned by the overpowering smell of the flowers. He had never felt the summer temperature drop so close to water-freeze, as micro-frogs and blue-crockets started up their haunting song of the early blue. He could not help but enjoy the walk, with so much for his senses to absorb, although thoughts kept intruding of what might have become of the Hjiretts, of his injured father at home, and of Teg waiting and worrying as she watched over their father.

In just over an hour, they were in striking distance of home, and the full extent of their circumstance became clear.

Since they had left the house, what seemed like a week had passed, but in reality it was just a few hours. No-one could prepare them, however, for the sight of the forest blocking their view ahead of the house, a long finger having reached out from the heart of the woods, as they had known them until this day, and touched their garden. Such an intrusion into their personal space was unheard of, and carried threat and outrage with it. The trees had moved, and not in a random way, nor in a steady line, but with deliberate, malicious foresight and direction. It was as if the forest itself had gained some sort of consciousness and was reaching out a hand to…if the Hjirett's experience was any guide, to crush and wipe away humans and their habitations; the revenge of the woods against the woodsmen and the creatures of the wood against the hunters.

'How are we going to get to them?' whispered Loty, although the trees far ahead would not be able to hear them, even if they had ears to do so. They were at least a ninety blibs away, and they could only just be seen in the deep blue gloom.

'Aiy! My dear one, Teg and Sniddy, Gvonly and Dalli need us now. We must find a way. Let me think. Let me think.' Mah stopped and pulled out her blade, regarding its keen edge in a new way.

She was a strong woman, and a good fighter, particularly when her family was under threat. She had come to a difficult decision, and took her son by the shoulder to ensure his attention and his obedience. She spoke to him slowly and deliberately, at some length. They looked a strange sight, under a deep blue sun; two humans huddled together, wearing eye-slit shields and baggy hats, their faces translucent with ant grease, shirts tight-buttoned at neck and wrist.

'You must do this for me,' she said, 'and also for your family. This plan must work, Loty.' She looked straight at him, injecting confidence into her voice. 'It must work.'

Potomah hugged him, kissed him once, tucking her long plait under her hat, and set off down-mercury, in the direction of the old forest itself. Loty had never seen her like this, as determined as any warrior of ancient Iole. Meanwhile, Loty started to hack pieces from tongue-bushes, geezer grass and anything else he could use to weave himself a disguise. As soon as he saw his mother disappear into the gloom of the trees he started to move, slowly, slowly, looking for the entire world like a clump of vegetation. Even the buzz-moths gathered around him in the hope of some food, as he had crushed ultra flowers into his pockets, just as Mah had told him, to complete the disguise. In this way he moved closer to the woods in a direct line with his house, thumb by thumb and toe by toe.

He fought against the urge to sneeze as the pollen dust flew off him, and made himself concentrate on the goal by counting to nine, taking a small step and resting, repeating this manoeuvre over and over again, for more than half an hour until he reached the trees which barred his way to the front door. Then, rather than risk discovery by taking a straight line, he circumnavigated the house and the trees until he had a good view of the drainpipe that sniggered up the back of the house, to the roof. It was only then that he saw the creatures running up and down the trunks of the nearest tree. As he watched, one of the Mafgherli leapt onto the wall of the house itself and tried the shutters with its sharp teeth, but these were made from the hardest and most resilient targa-wood and could not be damaged thus. Only he knew that there was one loose shutter on the first floor, covering one of his own bedroom windows. It was something that he should have fixed himself, or told his father about weeks ago, but now this was his one hope that might just save his life. Ever more cautiously, and anticipating discovery at any moment, he edged toward the drainpipe that led up the wall, past his bedroom window.

Once in position he waited for the sign, just as his mother had bade him. He was sweating now, despite the cold, and the ant grease was starting to melt and drip from his forehead. He hoped that it still offered protection, as he had no wish to escape being devoured by the Mafgherli and avoid being crushed by the trees, just to end up with weeping burns over his exposed skin and a lethal dose of radiation that would take another week to finish him off. It was way past blue now, and his skin was beginning to tingle through the disguise of leaves and twigs, and even through the tight-weave cloth hat he wore. He could smell burning as a few of the moths, which lived for just one hour, died as the radiation bit into them. They began to smoke and disintegrate.

He watched the Mafgherli through his slitted eye-screen, becoming increasingly active as the minutes ticked by, and trying out the defences of the house with more audacity. They tried to lift the roof slates, they prised away at the shutters with sticks, and they searched for drainage outlets, loose stones, airbricks, anything to gain them entry. Sometimes they 'spoke' in voices that squeaked into the ultrasonic range, and sometimes they stood on their back legs, pointed noses skywards, and listened as if awaiting their instructions from the forest itself.

Then came the noise that Loty was waiting for, and which sent every one of the creatures running for the front of the house. With a warrior's ear-piercing scream, Potomah charged out of the forest, her knife shining black with blood in the blue light, and a heavy bundle under her right arm. She drove the small creatures away by force of her charge, protecting herself and her bundle, and hacked a route through branch and body to her own front door. Teg, who had been listening to the events outside as they unfolded, opened the door a crack, to let in the bloodied and torn female, who had ripped such a path of destruction through the trees, and the limp bundle of rags she carried. Potomah fell into the room; she collapsed in a heap on the kitchen floor, and it was by no means clear, initially, whether the blood which was upon her belonged to herself or to the foes she had cut down on the way. Sniddy rushed to her from under the table where she had been curled up when Teg had gone to the door.

  'Mah! Mah! You're hurt!' and she cradled her mother's head in her hands.

It must be said that the mixture of grease, sweat, grime and blood on her mother's face was quite fearsome to behold. It was a moment or two before her mother knew whether she, herself, was badly hurt or not. She checked her limbs, her various aches and pains, touched her bloodied garments, and discovered that she was bruised and scratched, but no more, and immediately moved for the bundle she had carried through the forest. She had found the body of her son, Gvonly, hanging from the branch of a tree, hooked by his collar, unconscious but still alive. He was in a terrible state. He was badly burnt by the sun, and all of his fingers were missing from his left hand, presumably bitten clean off. At that moment, there was a sound of thudding as someone ran down the stairs and burst into the kitchen from inside the house; Loty had made it.

'Mah! Teg! Oh, Sniddy!' he exclaimed, quickly losing his joy at seeing them as he caught sight of his brother. 'I closed the shutter and checked it!' he quickly added, in answer to his mother's silent question.

'He is close to death,' said their mother, searching Gvonly's body for other signs of injury, finding long, dagger-like holes in his clothes, which had nicked his skin but had otherwise caused no great damage.

The tree had held him aloft by skewering his coat on thorn-like projections, but had held short of taking his life. 'And, Father, how does he lie?' she asked of Teg.

'He is sleeping. I sung to him for a while and I know that he will be okay, Mother. Don't worry, it is more urgent that we heal Gvonly.'

Loty raised the knife in his hand and threw it with deadly intent. It clattered off the kitchen wall, as he sprung to his feet. They turned to see a Mafgherli standing up on its rear legs in their kitchen, and Loty picked up the nearest kitchen knife to face it. The wretched creature just sat back down on its haunches and quivered with fear. Mah raised her arm to stay her eldest son from further violence.

'Enough! This one's not going to harm us.'

'It's been hurt, Mah,' said Teg, 'I sang to it, and it spoke to me. It means us no harm. It has shaken off the spell of the forest, and now it is as frightened of the creatures outside as we are. It begs us not to harm it further.

Her mother looked puzzled. 'No-one can understand the language of the Mafgherli. You cannot have heard!' she said. 'Most of it we cannot hear, let alone understand.'

But, even as she said this she knew that what her daughter said was true. Teg may not have the sight that was her own birthright, but she could hear things that no other person could, and her singing voice had a soothing, healing property, and brought peace and joy to those that let it inside them. She had never known Teg to tell a lie. She was someone on whom you could depend, even with your life.

At that moment there was a terrible noise, like an avalanche or rock fall outside, although there was no slope or snow to cause either of these. The deep, rumbling, scraping sound, which was the closest description from within the experience of those present, ended with an impact on the wall of the kitchen which caused dry daub to fall away in pieces and left an inward-folded dent. Something huge had struck the house, like the swipe of a giant club.
'The trees!' was all that Potomah needed to say.

The Mafgherli limped over to Teg and tucked itself under the protection of her arm. Sneddy burst into tears and clung to her mother, whilst Loty, still covered with twigs and dripping with dirty ant grease, looked at his mother as if to say 'so this is the end of our battle; this is how it ends'. Gvonly lay there, limp, all but lifeless, his blue-black skin looked grey; it was so dry and seared, where his face and hands had been exposed, and bloodied clothes torn and holed by his terrible adventure. His spirit was preparing to depart. In the midst of the turmoil and despair, only Teg sat there still and strong. She spoke.

'I know what to do.' Mah looked at her and saw how strong and serene her daughter had become.

Under her arm, the Mafgherli's long snout twitched and its bead-like eyes looked up at her as if in approval. It made a rasping squeak that sounded a little like a knife being scraped over a fire tile. It was speaking to Teg.

'Grandma used to tell us stories of the old times, about the higher levels. I always listened, Mah. I always listened to those stories, because somehow I knew that I was...one of the blessed.'

She found this hard to say, as it sounded so silly when spoken aloud. It was one thing to hear it in the speech of the Mafgherli, but quite another to announce it in front of her family. If only her father was here. As someone denied sight in this world, Teg suddenly found herself much better connected to worlds which lay just out of the sight of ordinary folk.

There was another huge impact between tree and house, as the giant's hammer struck again, this time high up, at roof level, and further round to the back of the house. The forest was angry. It had been tricked and defied too many times tonight, and now the midnight hour approached, it summoned its full strength and anger to crush them out of existence. Mah had already seen what they could do to a house, up at the Hjirett's place, given a little time.

'No-one has done this in living memory, Teg,' said her mother, looking at her with fresh eyes, and taking every word seriously. 'You know how dangerous it ever was to leave this level and travel on a soul-line. You may not reach your destination. If you do, you may not return. You may become one of the spirits, Teg.'

Potomah and Teg looked at each other and knew that there was no other choice. They could not run through the forest, not with Father on his bed and Gvonly fading away as they watched, not at this deadly hour of the night. They could not stay where they were. It was only a matter of time before the walls of the house were breached and they were overwhelmed with Mafgherli, crushed by the mighty trees of the forest, or struck down by the rays of the midnight sun. Outside, by now, the air would also be thick with the spores of exploding buzz-moths, and these too were instantly toxic to humans. Teg's plan was the only one left. The giant's hammer struck again, and there was the sound of glass shattering at the side of the building. The walls would not hold for long. There was another huge blow that shook the dust out of the roof, hard on the last, as the trees seemed to realise they could win, and focused their strength.

Teg took the Mafgherli and placed it on her lap, holding it tightly. It could hear the forest calling to it now, and it was afraid of being overtaken again by the anger, or of being torn apart if it resisted the destructive will of its own tribe. She leant across to Gvonly. 'Mother, please let me touch the blood of my brother.'

Without questioning, she felt her hand being held against his, and her skin was daubed with a mixture of sticky blood and fragments of bark that held on to his clothes and dusted him like a cloak. She tried to breathe slowly, withdrawing her mind, pulling in on herself, away from the noises, the smells and the fear of her situation, as the building shook twice more to the hammer-blows of the forest, and this time it seemed as if the continued noise of falling materials signalled that the roof had, indeed, been breached. Sniddy was crying and shouting for her mother. And, in the midst of this noise and destruction, Teg began to sing. Her song had no words that could be recognised, and the melody was none that they had ever heard before. It was an extraordinary song, not quite of this world, and it held them all in its ebb and flow.

The forest outside fell silent, and the Mafghleri clung to bark and leaf, straining to listen. Where it came from, Teg did not know, but she did know that it felt right for the moment, and it spread a protective orb of sound around the house for what seemed like a long time, until Teg collapsed in a heap, the Mafgherli too, like limp rags on the kitchen flagstones, and then the silence was total. Not a twig moved in the forest, and the peace bound them together, like a benign spell.

The first thing that Teg saw was her grandmother standing, smiling by the door. This was remarkable in that Teg had never been able to see anything, having been blind from birth. This was also remarkable, in that Teg immediately recognised the rather handsome woman as her grandmother, never having seen her or any other human before. This was a dream unlike any she had had before, which had all been dreams of her own, sightless world of touch and taste, sound and smell. Holding her hand was her brother, Gvonly, quite restored to health, and the Mafgherli was sitting quietly on her shoulder, its tail curled around her neck. Her grandmother spoke, 'Remember what to do, Teg! Remember the old tales!' She smiled, her presence fading away as she did so, and Teg stepped through the doorway into a featureless world of light and weightless disembodiment.

As they moved together, Teg noticed that bright rope-like strands of plasma trailed behind them, and she knew that this was a soul journey she was making, that they all were making. Their bodies had been left behind, and at any moment their soul-tethers could be broken, at which point there would be no return. The images they saw of one another were simply mind projections. Within the landscape of light there were brighter baubles, drifting past, and sometimes a whistling in their ears as a faded spirit passed them and tried for a moment to reach out and communicate. They were truly in the land of lost and fading souls, the place which had been much visited by the ancestors, who had built great things on the surface of Miraba by working their spells from the higher planes. Teg looked long and hard at her brother, Gvonly, seeing him for the first time. He smiled at her. This was a miracle, and she felt as if she could spend a thousand years in this place, just learning to use her eyes. As her vision cleared, more detail became visible, and she could see more and more of the things she could only have previously known by touch, smell or taste. This was a faded mirror-world of the one she knew, but one in which she felt powerful and whole. Whatever she did here could have untold effects in the world she had just left, and she realised that her mind was drifting and that she must get back to doing what she had intended, or risk losing her purpose entirely. The Old Ones spent years in training for this moment, with all of its risks and rewards, whereas Teg had to dive in, sink or swim!

The Mafgherli spoke to them in plain speech, which they were amazed to understand, 'You must sing to us, Teg! You must sing to Gvonly, as the poisons even now are battling to stop his heart. You must sing to me, like an angel, and reverse the terrible mutation that has fused us to the forest and now wreaks destruction upon your people.'

So they settled down to concentrate on the great task. In Teg's imagination there was a plane tree with bark of perfect silver, and leaves of sapphire. This represented the great forest. They sat facing one another as Teg began to sing. She did not know where the words came from, but only that they came from deep inside her. Her voice was full of grace and peace, and it flowed through the Mafgherli, who swayed from side to side, and through Gvonly, who closed his eyes and raised his hands in welcome. She sang until all of their tiredness was gone. She sang until she was the only one who could remember who they were, where they had travelled and where they were from. Then one by one they felt the pull of their soul-tethers, calling upon them to travel faster and faster, with great urgency, away from that place of peace, and back to the world they knew. Only, for Teg, it was too late because her soul had wondered and delighted at the gift of sight, and refused to return.

They took Teg's lifeless body, with its eyes that had never seen, and buried it deep in the forest. The Mafgherli lined the branches of the trees and sung to the funeral entourage in their strange voices, just at the edge of hearing. The forest was at peace, and all of the people of the homesteads and villages had travelled to thank Teg's family for their sacrifice and to farewell her spirit. The Hjiretts were there, having escaped the attack on their own house and fled over the Midlock to the nearest town. Many of the woodlanders and dwellers on the scrub had been less fortunate, and were themselves mourning members of their families, lost to the forest or to the Mafgherli. Several hundred stood now in the clearing, as great wheels of giant yellow flowers opened their petals and released sprays of nectar into the humid air. They all faced Dallimurgh, Teg's grieving father, as he began to speak.

'We are gathered here in the red of the morning to say goodbye to our daughter Teg, who saved us with her bravery and her foresight.' There was deep sadness and also pride in his words. 'Her sight was so much greater than ours, even though her eyes were blind in our world; now she is in a place where she can watch over us.'

Then, Gvonly spoke, seeming much older and wiser than his years, 'She made the decision not to return. She chose this path, and we must love her all the more for what she has done, and respect her choice. We are thankful that she is our sister. She will watch over us and keep us safe, from the next world.'

'She has saved the forest,' said Potomah, as Sniddy held tight to her hand, 'and all of us who live in and around the forest, the creatures of the forest, the lives of the hunters and the gatherers. Who knows how much destruction could have been caused if the change had gone unchecked? So, to Teg, our daughter, whose body is put to rest today, wherever you are, whatever you are doing....we thank you with all our hearts.'

At that moment every leaf seemed to rustle and every branch vibrate, as the forest shook to the wave front of some mysterious song. Every face looked up to the red sun and they too heard it, the sound of a distant voice singing, notes rising and falling in keys unknown and with beauty unimaginable. The sound was everywhere, inside them and around them. It was Teg. She was with them.

Sniddy, tried so hard to smile. So hard.

The Tiebreaker

A knocking was heard and the voices in the room settled at once. The long hall was filled with silence and anxiety for a moment, then the Soferex Dextra slowly stood. People listened intently as his voice echoed through the hall, making his opening statement. Begnarus began making notes.

He spoke of the current political situation. Iole, still being the main world power, was coming under rising pressure from other nations across Miraba. Countries like Fraxis and Ahila Fevia were making new discoveries constantly, and were rising in power. A particular threat was Tavura, with its vast land, which held many natural resources, and was increasing in wealth. It had begun trading with Fraxis and other nations, allowing it to rise in power even more. Along with its bad relations and competition with Iole there was actually a considerable threat of an invasion. Iole needed some way of staying ahead if it were to avoid this. The meeting rolled on from there. By the end, the Soferei had agreed to launch a new propaganda campaign, and Beignus sided with the idea of putting more into scientific research, though not seeing much in either.

Beignarus Previus was the tiebreaker of the monarchy. With his position of siding with the Soferex he agreed with in meetings, he was granted a lot of power, but he had been voted in by the aristocracy, so had a responsibility to make the right decision and not to abuse his power. He was quite an honest man who had always wanted to have a good influence, and had a good reputation amongst his colleagues, who thought of him as the epitome of chivalry. He had a wife and two children; a boy aged seven and a girl aged nine, and was generally pleased with his life. He was quite devoted to his responsibilities.

The next meeting Beignarus attended was quite a different one, a significant one. It had been about a week since the previous meeting, and the advisors of the Soferei had been thinking their ideas through of what was to be done. The Soferei sat on opposite ends of the table as usual, then the Soferex Sinistra stood. People were rather surprised at what he said, and listened curiously.

"After some thought and research, the decision of the left side has been made. On the far side of Miraba, stands Vicir, the lost continent. We have looked into this and decided there is potential in this land."

As he spoke, Beignarus thought it through. 'Out of the little that is known about this land, there is evidence of human life there. By exploiting this land, we will be exploiting the indigenous. Inevitably, we will mistreat them too if we are to achieve control. The expense of the moral outweighs the value of the economic profit. We must not go into Vicir'.

He could stop it happening only if it is opposed by the Soferex Dextra. As the Soferex Dextra stood, Beignarus's heart thumped against his ribs. The hope that he would oppose the Vicir act hung in Beignarus's mind as it was pressurised from all sides.

"After some thought and discussion with my advisor, I have made my decision on what it is right to do. As the current main world power, we need to secure our place. The appropriate solution is more research into what Fraxis is trying to discover. We have the advantage already, but putting our concentration to Vicir would put us into a state of vulnerability".

When he announced he did oppose it, the burden was released from Beignarus' mind and he was filled with a warm feeling of relief. The rest was easy. When his opinion was called for, he simply sided with the Soferex Dextra, who had opposed it for a different reason, but that didn't really matter. When the meeting ended, he left it with a feeling of relief, triumph and some tiredness. That day, he went home to his family.

He was greeted warmly by his wife and his children ran to the door to see him. He entered the house and was asked questions such as what had happened at work, by his wife, and he spoke a lot about it. They always admired him as a good man.

He left for the palace of the Soferei the next morning. As they entered the drive, he felt slightly nervous in anticipation of what might happen. He thanked the driver and began walking. When he arrived, he was greeted by a messenger who had a concerned and slightly hesitant look about him. He took a deep breath and began apprehensively.

"I have bad news for you." He began, in a nervous voice. "While you were away, we received news of the death of an advisor, the advisor of Soferex Dextra. The aristocrats are nominating a new one right now".

Beignarus was taken aback. "Is he much different? What are his opinions on the Vicir act?" Beignarus began to panic.

"We don't know much about him", said the messenger.

Beignarus pushed past and began hurrying to find more news. No one seemed to know. 'It's fine.' He thought to himself. 'He will be elected by the same people, so should have similar opinions, and there isn't likely to be any dramatic changes.' Beignarus calmed himself down and tried to forget the matter. He carried on that day as normal.

The next day, as he was entering the palace, he saw a stranger who stood next to a colleague. The stranger was a plump and confident looking man. He stood there, nodding and looking around with a satisfied look on his face. The colleague spotted Beignarus through the crowd, jerking his eyebrows up, and led the stranger over to him.

"Beignarus!" he bellowed. He pushed through the mass of people, dragging the stranger behind him. "I don't suppose you've met the new advisor!" A wave of anxiety hit Beignarus. "This is Faenator Inexor".

The advisor greeted Beignarus warmly, but formally. Beignarus looked at him. Already he began studying his traits. He seemed rather smug, probably about his new job. He appeared very pompous, and seemed to look upon everyone else superciliously. "You wouldn't mind showing Faenator around would you?" asked the colleague.

Beignarus cringed slightly. "Of course not!" he said, putting on a smile. The colleague left. The new advisor studied the room. There was silence for a short while.

"So, you're the tie breaker?" he asked, though not really interested.

"Yes" said Beignarus, "How do you feel, being a new advisor?

"Pleased." He said, "I've just bought a new house in the right hand side. This new job means I can afford a lot more."

"And what about the job itself?" asked Beignarus,

"Yes, I am looking forward to running a few more things. Things are going to get a lot better".

As they continued talking, Beignarus began disliking him more and more. He had the attitude of a businessman towards politics. 'He seems only to care about making his life better,'

Beignarus thought, 'He could be a drawback to the monarchy'. Beignarus became increasingly worried.

His worries were proved to be well founded in the next Soferei meeting. There was a different atmosphere in the hall this time, a slight sense of hostility. The Soferei prepared to make their opening statements. The Soferex Dextra looked up across the table. He had an unsure look in his eyes. He stood up. Hesitantly, he began to talk. "During this meeting," he cleared his throat, "I wish to discuss plans concerning the Vicir act."

This shocked Beignarus. He suddenly became alert and was filled with adrenaline.

"We have decided against previous ideas and feel that colonising Vicir is necessary, if we are to remain in our position amongst other nations".

Beignarus was stunned. The light of hope in his mind was quenched. Vicir would be invaded. Why had he changed his mind? Things were going fine! 'It must be the new advisor. He will have thought it would benefit him. We will be capitalising on people, taking what is theirs! Ruining them! He has led us to this just for himself.'

The meeting seemed to draw to a close quickly. Thoughts flashed through his mind. 'Perhaps the Soferex Sinistra will oppose it. Maybe it will be okay,' though he knew it was hopeless. Soferex Sinistra stood with a slightly puzzled but satisfied grin. Beignarus could only watch him announce that he favoured the act. He was powerless. He left the meeting with a feeling of emptiness. He reached for the door with a shaking hand. As he left the palace, he looked across the room to see Advisor Inexor standing at the other end with a smug, pompous look about him, waiting for the news. Beignarus felt hate towards him, nothing more. The same feeling filled him for the whole journey home.

When he arrived at home, he was greeted in the usual, delighted manner, but he didn't feel in the right mood. He greeted them with a smile, but instead of spending much time with them, he went to sleep early. He felt sickness and defeat only. The fate of a whole people had been decided and he had been powerless. He had lost on this front and could only watch helplessly as the people of Vicir had their way of life torn apart.

He woke up the next morning with the same dark shadow hanging over him. 'I must forget it', he thought, 'There's no use letting the thought oppress my mind. I have lost this battle, and must move on. Economically, I will benefit from the Vicir act.' That thought made him feel sick, but he was an optimist. At least he tried to be.

When he arrived at the palace, he saw Advisor Inexor hurrying towards him. "What did you think of the meeting the other day?" he asked with a self-satisfied look about him.

Beignarus Previus said nothing.

"Listen, there will soon be another meeting, I have spoken with the Soferex Dextra and if you side with him on his financial restructuring, you will receive even more benefit," said Inexor.

Beignarus Previus thought this through as he left. What would the Soferex Dextra say, and would he go along with it? When the Soferex Dextra stood up in the meeting, he listened curiously. With the same unsure look on his face, he began to speak.

He eventually concluded with, "It is my belief that by increasing the pay given to politicians here, giving them privatised companies and the previously mentioned changes, we can increase loyalty and improve the way our monarchy is run".

The Soferex Sinistra opposed it, then it was down to the tie breaker. Beignarus Previus thought it through; the new money, the new power, a better life altogether. He imagined living in a larger house, with him and his family enjoying life more. He imagined the things he would own, the power he would have. He disagreed with the statement, but did it really matter? 'Things seemed bad, but they are going to improve now', he thought. Slowly, he rose to his feet. He took a deep breath and smiled. "I favour the change in system", he announced.

He left feeling satisfied, though quite unsure about what he had done. He went to find Faenator Inexor, who greeted him cordially. "I favoured the change", he told him.

"Great! I knew you would." He replied. "Everything is going to improve for us now. You will be much richer; you will have your own businesses."

"Yes, I suppose so."

"You made the right decision"

Beignarus Previus walked off feeling reassured. As he left the building, a messenger ran up to him.

"With the new changes, you have been given a new title. Sequor Previus," he said formally, and handed him a tag. As he walked away, Previus looked at the tag, rubbed it until it shined, and grinned as he gazed down the long path.

It was early summer, and the landscape shone in shades of orange. Sequor Previus sat in the front end of the palace. It had been a few months since he received his new title.

"So how are things going for you?" a colleague asked him.

"Everything's going well, the insurance company at the back end of Iole is in good business, and of course, the new building project in Vicir."

"And what about at home, how's your family?"

"Great, I've added another extension to the house, I'm sure they love it."

"Have you seen them recently?"

"Not since our company bought out Probus, I've been quite busy recently."

In the next meeting, the Soferei discussed the rising threat of an invasion. He strode in proudly and sat casually in his seat. They discussed whether to improve relations with Tavura, to begin trading with Ahila Fevia, to capitalise more on their lands in Vicir or to prepare for a war. When he left, he met Faenator Inexor.

"What was the meeting like?" Faenator asked,

"Fine, I favoured tougher methods in controlling lands in Vicir, which should ensure my lands are secure",

"It's great isn't it? We have so much power and money, what more could we want?"

"It's marvellous."

As Sequor Previus left, he began to think. The two of them were very different. He realised he didn't really believe in what he did, but was convinced by what he said. He remembered how he had viewed him before, then thought of what he had done in Vicir. He had almost forgotten about that. He imagined what life was like for the indigenous. Then he comforted himself. 'They will probably be fine. It wasn't my fault we went there anyway, the Soferei decided it. I was merely trying to benefit from it'. Then he thought of his family, their value in his life. He decided to visit them.

He arrived home later that day. His wife and children greeted him delightedly. He spent time with his children, then spoke with his wife.

"Why haven't you visited us recently?" she asked,

"I have been busy" he replied,

"The children have missed you. How has work been?"

"Better every day. The plantations in Vicir are more secure than ever. We now have about fifty armed guards in each and they think the indigenous are becoming a bit more intimidated"

"Yes. Would you like a drink?"

"No thanks. You seem uncomfortable. Is something wrong?"

"No, no."

"Good. Are you sure?"

"Yes, well, it's just that," she began hesitantly; "Do you not think you're going a bit too far?"

"Why?" He asked agitatedly,

"The way they are treated, by Iole."

"What do you mean?" He demanded,

"I've heard about it. Perhaps you should be a bit more, merciful."

"Merciful?" He became angry. "I've been doing all this for you! So you can have a better life! So you can be happier! And this is what you say!"

"Perhaps it would have been better, for them, if you had, not gone this far."

"This is how you thank me? Are you not grateful? I've worked hard! I've succeeded! Just look at how far we've come! And you blame me for taking that?"

"I'm sorry"

He dismissed what she said, and left.

He remained bothered and irate. He reassured himself by backing up what he had said in his mind, though really, he knew he was only in denial. He knew she was right, and that he had made wrong decisions. His morale had hit a wall. He lay there with mixed feelings, unsure what to do. 'I have travelled too far down this road to turn back.' He could only wait, to see what the next day held for him.

He left for work in the morning while his family were asleep. He thought back to the other night and laughed. He had been tired, and thought too deeply. That's what he put it down to. 'This is just how things work. I have not committed any crimes by doing what I have done in Vicir. My wife was wrong. She doesn't understand politics. She doesn't see how things work or what is necessary. It's not just a world in which we can all be nice to one another, that's just not how it works,' he thought.

These thoughts grew more and more adamant in his mind. For the next few days, in the palace, he continued as normal, unchanged by the events at home. The suspicion of an attack grew more and more popular a subject in meetings, and he had learnt the best ways to capitalise on the options and benefit himself from it. One incident occurred when the Soferex Dextra refused to comply with Faenator Inexor, who he accused of making bad political decisions and letting national issues slip by. He said he had doubted him from the start, but Faenator Inexor eventually convinced him otherwise and the matter passed. Things went quite smoothly for a while after. But the Soferei's fears had not been unfounded. On a night in mid summer, the whole palace awoke. News had arrived that a large army from Tavura had landed on the coast. Panic arose. People began talking. Trepidation filled the air. The Soferei prepared to speak with their advisors. Sequor Previus was caught in the midst of this. He thought about what may happen. This was serious. They were very vulnerable with all their concentration on Vicir. 'I should have been more careful', he thought, 'I need to stop concentrating on my own benefits for a while and look for the best way for our country to get out of this'. He had not expected a war this dangerous. 'Supposing we lost the war', he thought, 'What would happen then? We would be conquered. We would become slaves. All the power that I have built up so much, that has cost time, effort, the lives of people in Vicir, that I value so highly, gone.'

That made him quake at the very thought. He would do whatever he could to stop the invaders, no matter how many more lives it would cost.

He was driven by determination in the meetings to come. The Soferei, disagreeing a lot as usual, would discuss whether to agree a truce with Tavura, or to continue fighting, to which he would conclude with something along the lines of, "We have too much to give up and must not surrender our power and global status".

His family were also put under stress. They were caught up in the events more than he was. His wife sat at home talking to his children. The last remnants of dark blue in the sky were fading into darkness. His children asked questions about where he was, to which she would respond; "Working hard for us and for our country". They looked up to him as much as they had always done. It had been a fairly ordinary day and they were going through a normal routine, but they were stopped by a faint sound of rumbling and distant screams. She ran over to the window and was caught by a sight she had long feared. In the distance, a dark mass spread across the hills, surrounded by a red glow. She knew what it was. It was an army from Tavura, a raid, and they were unprotected. She paused in shock for a few seconds, and then reacted. She had to make decisive actions. She ran to her children, grabbing a few essentials on the way, food, water, ant grease, and then began to hurry them out of the house. The children were caught up in the confusion and panicked. They hurried out and she bundled them behind a hedge. The mass of people was still far away. She estimated that the sun would be emitting harsh rays at that moment. At mid summer, the levels of radiation would be extremely high, and the rays at midnight would be very dangerous. Although covered with night screen from head to toe, they needed to find shelter. After peering out and scanning the landscape, she helped her children up and led them on towards the forest. When they arrived, she looked back at their house. 'What will happen to us now?' She thought.

She looked around. The land was covered in a layer of smoke. Houses burned, people scattered in every direction, screaming, as the army flooded in. She began to lose hope. She looked over at her children. They sat, talking, worried looks on their faces. As they sat in the undergrowth of the forest, she heard the sounds of feet treading across the leaves. She grabbed her children and pulled them behind a tree. They crouched there, wide-eyed, holding their breath. As she listened, the footsteps grew louder, then stopped. She closed her eyes, tensing, her nerves on edge. She heard a sharp whisper. She held her children tightly. An agitated, Tavuran voice began talking, then grew rapidly to a shout.

Sequor Previus awoke to the sound of footsteps. As he prepared for work and began to leave, he caught sight of a stressed looking man pacing outside his office door. "Come in then", he shouted. The man lifted his head as if shocked. He seemed slightly frightened. He opened the door tentatively, clutching some papers. "The Tavurian invasion has advanced further." He began, "They have taken a lot of land in the south. I am sorry to have to tell you that they have taken the area around your house". At first, he didn't quite believe it. He couldn't. Then a feeling inside him grew into outrage. "My family were in there. Are they safe?"

"We haven't received any reports that they have been seen. I am sorry, but We don't think there is much hope of finding them." Previus was silent.

"Are they sure?"

"The house has been seen. It was burned to the ground."

"There must be some chance"

"I'm afraid that we've done all we can"

"No! Tell them to send more search parties! If there is any chance of them being alive I want it taken!"

The man left. Previus paced up and down the room, then sat at his desk, his hands clutching his head. He waited nervously for any news for the next few days, even though he knew it was hopeless. The Tavurian army approached closer to the centre each day. Tension grew to the extent that people began fleeing Iole. Eventually, so did he. He left for Vicir a few days later. The vehicle that would take him to the coast waited outside the centre. He left with a few belongings. On the way, he stopped to look back. He felt some unexpected anticipation of a new life, but was reminded of the same feeling of emptiness as before. His wife and children were dead. He dropped to his knees, tortured by the grief, and screamed. As he crossed the long, tall stone bridge above the deep gorge, he faced the strong current of wind and lent over the side. He felt neither fear, nor amazement.

Days later, he arrived in Vicir. He awoke as the boat dragged to a halt. He had tried to put everything behind him, but nothing could raise his mood. As he left the boat, he saw an unexpected sight. Scattered across what had used to be a clean but inhabited coast, were Iolian buildings. There was a lot of ruin below them. What caught him the most were the natives. They sat along the beach, wearing Iolian clothes, eating Iolian food. They were imprisoned in an Iolian lifestyle. A long queue led to an Iolian alcohol stall, with what used to be a large native hut below it. As he walked down, faces rose to glare at him. He saw one man crying and drinking. He went inland and found one of his plantations. Two armed guards stood outside. There was a wrecked hut and two dead bodies to the right; a woman and a child. Previus couldn't bear to see it. He turned, and thought for a while. Up to this point, he had been feeling sorry for himself, now, he only felt disgust. He had caused this. It was his fault. He had been in denial, until he saw what he had done. He walked to the coast, feeling shocked. Thinking only of money, he had capitalised on land, capitalised on resources, and inevitably, capitalised on people. He had been ambitious and aimed higher all his life, but had only seen things in one way, but in all situations, wherever, for one man to rise above, others must fall below. As he walked, some skinny natives sneered at him, and he accepted it. He approached the drink stall, paid, and then carried a bottle away. An Iolian advanced towards him with a message from one of the boats. He didn't really listen to what he said, but simply dismissed him. He drained the bottle, then tossed it out into the sea.

Magical Fire Service

Hi, I'm Imohann, but everyone just calls me Im. I come from Rakour. I used to live in one of the cities- Pluer. I was happy there, I was normal.

I am a traveller, a wizard. I discovered it when I was caught in a fire three years ago.

Unfortunately, I was far from home, with my friends, when the other fire struck, the fire that orphaned me.

My grandparents on my mum's side were the only relatives I had left. So I was abandoned in the village they lived in. It was okay for the first day but then I went to school, everyone was nice at first, but on the first day a school was hit by another fire - it seems that all the worst events in my life start with a fire.

I was one of the first out and as I turned to see the pillar of smoke rising from the building I realised that this was not a drill.

As people were pouring out of the building and staring to panic, I sat down calmly and closed my eyes. I did get a few funny looks but they didn't know I was a traveller yet.

And then I was on another level – I poured a small amount of water over the school, completely drenching it and putting out the fire. I suppose that I thought everyone would be pleased, but when I came back to my body people were staring at me as if I had just started the fire, rather than putting it out.

"Have you never seen magic before?" I asked.
Nobody answered; they just shifted their eyes from me.
"It's not something to the scared of," I pleaded.

I took a step forward and they shrank back.

"The only thing travellers are good for is spirit mining" one of the boys said with pure hatred in his voice. With tears filling my eyes, I fled.

For the next few weeks the only people in the whole village who would even meet my eyes were my grandparents and it hurt. It hurt having no one to talk to, no one to hang out with, and no one to even look at me. In the end I gave up. I approached my grandma, tear stained and in despair.

"I can't do this. I can't stay here."

"I know it's hard but where else can you go?"

I had given this great thought and decided that I needed a complete change.

"Iole. There are lots of wizards there," I told her. I had learnt Iolian at school, so that would help.

She tried to convince me to stay but with no success, I just couldn't stay there. So that's how I ended up on a ship in the middle of the sea when a failed wind experiment hit and caused a storm. It was terrible, I'd heard about some of the failed experiments, but usually all that happened was that swimmers had slightly rougher waters than expected or things were blown away, but this was an extremely rough storm. I was swept overboard and clung to a nearby barrel, as I watched my vessel of escape sink.

I drifted for hours, clinging on as hard as I could until I washed up on the shore. I crawled up the beach away from the waves and collapsed. The next thing I knew was a woman standing over me, shaking me.

"You're awake! Can you walk?" the woman asked me.
I checked my legs, they felt fine but I couldn't be sure as they were so cold.

"I think so." I managed to whisper. My throat was on fire.

"Good, because we need to get inside quickly," I glanced up and saw she was right, the sun was blue.

With her help I managed to stagger to her house just in time for her to close blinds for the night. She gave me some dry clothes to change into and a bowl of soup that she had cooked before she had spotted me. The house was just at the top of the beach, so she had a clear view of the place, which was lucky for me.

After eating the soup and changing into the clothes, I settled down to sleep in the cosy, fire-lit cottage. The clothes were way too big for me, with the sleeves hanging down passed my hands, and the trousers threatening to trip me up if I tried to walk, but they helped me re-gain feeling in my limbs.

When I awoke, some time must have passed as it was mid-afternoon. The woman was bustling round the cottage but she stopped and went to the pot over the fire when she saw I was awake. She handed me a bowl of soup, then sat down.

"I'm Lidia. Who are you?" she asked in what I recognised as Iolian.

"Imohann," I replied shyly.

"So how did you end up half drowned on the beach?"

She listened in silence as I told my story in stuttering Iolian, glad of the little I knew.

"You poor, poor thing!" she exclaimed when I had finished, "At least you did end up in Iole."

I stayed with her for two weeks, in that time I ate loads of soup, you'd think it was all she ate (actually it was) and my Iolian improved considerably. We decided that I should head for the city of the Soferei. So I left with a map, a spare set of clothes (borrowed), a blanket (also borrowed), some food and money Lidia had given me – that was all I owned.

It took weeks, getting lifts on wagons from kind people, when I could, and walking when I couldn't. I slept in a barn or spare room of the people I passed, some people even let me stay for free, as I had little money but I would die sleeping in the open, in the midnight sun's deadly gaze.

Finally as I was walking I saw the city wall, with its split down the middle, which divided the place into Sinistra and Dextra, separate domains of the twin kings, the soferei. It had been over a month, I think, but I had lost track of the days in the muddle of walking and riding. I was beginning to worry, as Lidia's money was running out. By the end of the day I had reached the city.

As I stepped through the wall, I was overcome by the flood of sights, sounds even smells, which I had never seen, heard or smelt before. There were people rushing everywhere, a mix of voices calling to one another, I'm surprised they could even hear the person standing next to them. It took me awhile to navigate the crowded, twisting roads to Lidia's sister – Tania's house.

When I got there a woman who looked like Lidia opened the door. She listened in silence, like Lidia had, while I explained who I was, what had happened and why I was there.

"You'd better come in then," she said after I had finished explaining and she stepped aside so I could enter.

The house was very different from Lidia's cluttered cottage, everything was in its right place and there was enough room. In Lidia's cottage there was not much space as the clutter was everywhere.

Tania led me upstairs to the spare bedroom that was to become mine. It was a sweet little room, with light blue walls and a thick lilac carpet. There was a simple bed in one corner and a chest of drawers on the other side of the room. I placed my bag on top of the chest of drawers then went back with Tania.

In the kitchen, she started cooking something that smelled and tasted delicious. I had no idea what it was as it wasn't like anything I'd had at home.

After a few days, I went to the travellers' palace, following the directions Tania had given me. We'd decided it was the best place for me to go.

It was a massive palace, where travellers could come to use and develop their skills. I thought I'd never find my way round it. They welcomed me in there, I felt like I fitted in, even in Pluer I had never fitted in properly.

I work there now, but I still live with Tania. I'm part of the fire service; we put out any fires from the comfort of our room in the palace. I still don't know my whole way round, but it now seems smaller on the inside, than the outside.

Maybe the fires weren't so bad.

Food Fatality in Fertile Lands

Food coming from the fertile lands was yesterday reported to be infected with disease.

Gallosen gastromes, a fungus capable of giving the consumer the disease Gastrolesen, was found in products coming directly

from the Fertile Lands. Farmers claim not to know how this fungus may have got to their crops. The Food Research Society suspects the *Gallosen* may have got into the fertiliser that was made for the farmers in Gosber. Gosber's dung control facility had a spill a few weeks ago, and this may have been how the Gallosen may have made it into the crops. Tristus grain is the main crop to be infected. Citizens of Iole are advised to not eat or use any products containing this. These products are currently being taken off the market stalls.

Other crops do not contain *Gallosen* in high enough amounts to cause harm. However, there is also fear that this chemical contamination will cause financial difficulties in the fertile lands. Markets are already demanding a fresh stock of uninfected Tristus, and the fertile lands are struggling to produce this.

Consumer warning:

Intake is fatal: Your stomach will fill with gas and you swell up until you explode. This will only be cured if you roll in the multicoloured sand until you have no swelling, and this must be within less than 19 hours after intake (23 hours for children 5 – 16, 13 hours for babies, 11 for pregnant women, 7 for those with pre-existing illness and 2 for the elderly over 90 (over 100's will die on intake) Warning: These are only estimated times, you may just die. Extremely luckly people may survive.

Death rate 97%. Full recovery rate 0.5%.

The Lost Continent

It was becoming incredibly hard to see out over the foggy horizon of the murky waters, but Venaliter was certain. He had just seen the very edge of a shore he had never, in his entire 20 years of serving as the Soferei Sinistra, encountered before. He sailed onwards into the mist, peering behind him every now and then to check that no one could be following him. Then he saw it properly. There, in the middle of the sea, was the undiscovered country, the fabled land. He had found the lost continent of myth and legend. He had found Vicir.

Not much had changed in the running of this country in the world of Miraba in recent years. As it always had been, the land of Iole was ruled over by twin Soferei, Sinistra and Dextra. The current Soferei Sinistra was named Venaliter, a tall and bony man, greasy and crooked in his smile. He hadn't always been like that though. From a very young age he had been keen to rule over Miraba along with his brother, with whom he got on so well. He had just announced his engagement to the noble-born Suavis, who was as intelligent as she was beautiful, but he seemed somewhat distant and was no longer helpful and kind to the poor.

The current Soferei Dextra on the other hand, was the more peaceful of the two. His name was Potestas, and was as kind and gentle as he was powerful. He was short and bald, with a long and flowing brown cape that reached out to everyone.

These days the two Soferei, like most brothers, didn't always get along so well with each other. The two very rarely met, making sure they only convened when they had to, but sent spies daily to watch each other's actions. Usually these spies found nothing interesting or unusual in each of the Soferex' everyday behaviour, and therefore had nothing interesting to report back to their masters. But today was not a normal day. Today was different.

As usual, Potestas had sent his trusted advisor and right hand man, Obeodiens, to spy on Venaliter. Although he had never found anything interesting or unusual in Venaliter's behaviour to report back to his master, Obeodiens was always willing to do his master's bidding and felt honoured to do so.

He found Venaliter in his throne room as usual, accompanied by his right hand man, Geminlateral. Obeodiens had never liked Geminlateral, and not just because Geminlateral always spied on his master. Geminlateral didn't look entirely honest, as if he had something to hide, a kind of hidden agenda. But something was different this morning. Geminlateral wasn't off in Prosperitas spying on Potestas. Instead, he was whispering softly to his master in the corner of the throne room, turning round every couple of seconds as if he was scared of being watched. Obeodiens couldn't hear what they were saying, but decided to follow Geminlateral, instead of Venaliter, seeing as he was being more suspicious in his behaviour.

Geminlateral and Venaliter parted ways outside the room, Venaliter going left, whilst Geminlateral sneaked right. "What could he be up to?" thought Obeodiens, following at a distance.

Geminlateral took a few turns into various different hallways, and then went in the direction of Suavis' living quarters. "What could he want with Venaliter's betrothed?" thought Obeodiens, rather puzzled.

He tried to follow but the door was locked. He used a bit of old-fashioned magic to quietly unlock the door. Although his master was one of the great leaders of the movement, Obeodiens wished that scientific progress would just stay still. He was scared of what might happen if another massive discovery like the tuning fork occurred. He peeked through the keyhole of the room. There was Geminlateral and Suavis and they were...no! Geminlateral wouldn't betray his master like that. But he had. He wasn't sure, but for a split second, he was certain Geminlateral was looking right at him. Knowing that if he continued to stay outside the room, he would be seen and that Geminlateral and Suavis would probably spend a long time in there, he decided to start the long journey back to Prosperitas at the other end of Iole.

Once he was sure that Obeodiens had left, Geminlateral decided to tell Suavis of Venaliter's plans. You see, Geminlateral wasn't loyal like Obeodiens, he would betray anyone to get what he wanted, even the people who loved him.
"Geminlateral, my sweet love! Come closer!" whispered Suavis sweetly, as Geminlateral went over to the door and locked it. He came over to her and lay down beside her.

Suavis stared at him for a minute and then frowned.

"What is wrong my love? Is something on your mind?" she inquired.

Geminlateral thought for a moment, then asked: "Why do you love Venaliter?"

"I do not." answered Suavis sighing heavily. "I only want his money and power; otherwise I care not for him."

"Then we are much alike." he whispered softly in her ear, as he carefully slipped a blunt knife out of his pocket and into his hand.

When he got back to Prosperitas, Obeodiens immediately rushed to tell his master about Geminlateral's shocking affair with Venaliter's betrothed Suavis, and the odd and secretive behaviour of Venaliter himself. Potestas was shocked by Suavis' behaviour, yet intrigued by what Venaliter might be plotting. "All I heard..." explained Obeodiens, "Was Venaliter explaining to Geminlateral that he had made a discovery that would revolutionise our world forever."

"Well." mumbled Potestas, "He better not make a scientific discovery bigger than the tuning fork incident of last year or we're in trouble. Follow Geminlateral again tomorrow, I want to know what they're up to..."

The next day, Obeodiens rushed to Pax to find out what Venaliter and Geminlateral were hiding, only to overhear something shocking. They were already in the throne room, talking animatedly when he got there. He listened intently to what he could, but the constant hum from the palace kitchens was almost deafening and kept blocking out the sound of their speech.

" I can...finally tell you...discovered...island...vision...I...only Soferei...I could...I must...assassinate...his...and...Vicir!"

'Vicir'. The word that shocked him the most.

The land of myth and legend, that would bestow infinite power upon anyone who discovered it. Had Venaliter found it? Surely not? But if he had found it, then he had to warn Potestas! Was he going to assassinate Potestas to ensure his complete power over the fabled land? Quite shaken and confused by what he had overheard, Obeodiens began to make his way out of the building, down the corridor, picking up speed as he went, eventually braking into a run. He was nearly at the entrance of the palace. He had to get out of there before someone noticed him. However, as he passed through the corridor he accidentally caught an ancient ornamental vase on his cloak, which came crashing to the floor.

Venaliter stopped talking abruptly. He poked his head round the door, seeing no person, but spying the shattered vase, scattered across the floor. He walked back over to where his trusted advisor stood.

"We have been overheard." He snarled, turning to Geminlateral. "It must be Obeodiens. Potestas always sends him to spy on us. Follow him, and kill him. We cannot have Potestas learn of our plans, it is too risky."

Geminlateral obeyed and ran out of the building after Obeodiens, spotting him quickly then following him at a safe distance until they reached the stage-post where he boarded the wagon along with Obeodiens, eager to follow his master's wishes, although considering how he might be able to change the situation to his advantage...

When Obeodiens got off the wagonette he had the disturbing sensation that he was being followed. The cold breeze edged up the back of his spine, sending a chill throughout the whole of his body. He started to walk towards the gold-brick alley, slowly at first, then getting ever faster as the chilling breeze got colder and colder, and closer and closer to him. Suddenly, a knife leapt to his neck.
"You heard us, didn't you, slave?" hissed the voice of Geminlateral.

"No...." Obeodiens squealed. "I don't know....what you mean...."

"Yes you do slave. You were lurking outside the throne room. You overheard what we said about Vicir." He tightened his grip of the knife on Obeodiens' neck. "You were also spying on me and Suavis weren't you slave?" He drew blood. It was almost like a statement rather than a question.

"You'll pay for this." Obeodiens squealed again.

"No." he replied. "You will." The knife made a sudden movement.

Potestas was beginning to get concerned that Obeodiens hadn't yet returned, when he was visited by a very pleased looking

Geminlateral.
"What are you doing here? Where is my servant?"

"Dead. Venaliter caught him spying on us, and sent me to kill him. He planned to tell you my master's secrets."
Potestas was confused.

"Well your master seemed to be acting rather suspiciously recently and anyway I see you spying on me all the time, but do I send Obeodiens to kill you?" screamed Potestas. "GUARDS! Lock the doors!"

The guards did as requested but glanced nervously at Geminlateral.
"Why are you here? Do you expect to live? What have you come to tell me?" boomed Potestas.
Strangely, without any hesitation whatsoever, Geminlateral told Potestas all that he knew about Vicir and Venaliter's plans for it.
Potestas was shocked.
"If Vicir is real and Venaliter plans to rule over it alone, this means war! I will not stand for this!"

Geminlateral started edging towards the door, forgetting it was already locked.
"You're not going anywhere until you tell me where Vicir is!" shouted Potestas.

Geminlateral put his hand in his pocket and pulled out a quill and parchment. Shaking, he drew a rough sketch of the location of Vicir, just as Venaliter had described it to him, and handed it to Potestas.

"Perfect." said Potestas. "Guards, lock him up!"

"No!" squealed Geminlateral. "Please, have mercy, Sir! I mean no harm!"

"Handcuff him and sling him on my ship. I can't have him locked up here whilst I'm at sea, Venaliter might try to rescue him. I'll take him with me to Vicir," Potestas walked towards the door, "but first I have a meeting to attend."

Potestas had sent a messenger to find Venaliter then went to the meeting room to wait for him. He couldn't believe that Venaliter was so greedy that he would want to rule the hidden land alone and wield the largest amount of money and power Miraba could offer. Could he be?
The other person that Potestas had sent for – the tie- breaker, Cuberus, a merry yet rather plump man, entered the room.

"What seems to be the problem o' Soferex Dextra?" asked the polite and calm tie breaker, bumbling towards Potestas.

"The Sinistra, Venaliter has found the fabled country of Vicir and plans to seize it and rule it on his own, thus inheriting great riches and the most powerful position in the democracy of Iole!"

Venaliter entered the room, eyes glinting, hands in his pockets, yet again hiding something.

"Sit down." requested the tie breaker. Venaliter reluctantly sat down. "Now I know you must be feeling heartbroken at the tragic death of your beloved..."

"I care not for her!" spat Venaliter. "There is only one thing that I do care for and will always care for! And that is Vicir!"

"Right. I understand," said Cuberus, calmingly, "and that is what we are here to discuss – Vicir. The fabled land, the lost continent, if you will. That land cannot be walked alone."

"What are you trying to say, great oaf?" snarled Venaliter, spitting again.
"This could be the start of a great, new Miraban Age. We could all live with no more problems and no more suffering. It could enhance the lives of all of us! And you could be the rulers to start it! Both of you! We live not ruled by one leader, but two equal leaders, one for each half and that is how it should always stay! That is the way it should be!"

"It doesn't matter if it always stays like that." snarled Venaliter. "The people are blind, they care not."

"You cannot rule Vicir alone. I will not permit it." Cuberus said calmly.

"Then I'll force you to give your permission."

Venaliter stood up, circling the chairs where Potestas and Cuberus sat. "You cannot do this...This...means war. Iole will fall."

In a split second, the object in Venaliter's pocket was revealed, and he thrust the blade straight into the tie-breaker's heart. Cuberus fell to the floor with a thud. Potestas stood up, edging towards the door.

And with that the only thread binding Iole to peace was cut.

Potestas stood looking out across the vast and prosperous land of Iole, at the top of his highest tower. He feared the future. The trust between the two halves of the country had been broken and it was all his fault. If he hadn't sent Obeodiens to spy on Venaliter, Obeodiens wouldn't be dead, and he wouldn't have known about the hidden land. But Potestas knew he couldn't change the past. He looked down at the map. If Venaliter wanted war then that's what he would get. He gathered his belongings and went down to the docks to prepare his ship.

Potestas boarded his mighty sailing vessel and headed north to find the fabled land. He had gathered his army of over 1000 men, looking forward to the fight, all prepared to fight for their Soferex, even prepared to die for him. Potestas himself was also prepared to die, but not to kill. He could not bring himself to imagine killing his own brother. He also knew that if he did kill his brother, it was Miraban law that he must die too, but was it worth it? To destroy such a changed man, a corrupt force like Venaliter? Potestas' thought processes were interrupted by Fidelis, one of his most faithful servants. "Sir! I think we're here!" he shouted with enthusiasm.

Potestas gazed up at the magnificent isle that lay before him. Acre upon acre of luscious rainforest, a gigantic mountain, and long beaches glistening with golden sands met his eyes.
"It's beautiful..."

A guard interrupted his trail of thought.
"Sir, what should we do with Geminlateral?"

Potestas thought for a moment.
"Leave him locked up here. I cannot trust him. He would only complicate things."

Potestas disembarked from the ship. "My loyal men! Explore this incredible land for me and find Venaliter's men. If they attack you, I give you permission to fight back. But don't kill an innocent man. I will go find Venaliter..."

Potestas' men obediently set off into the rainforest.

Venaliter was up on the mountain, looking down at the golden beach in awe. He suddenly spotted Potestas' ship and had an idea for how he could easily beat Potestas.
"This will be easier than I thought..."he muttered.

He started to clamber back down the mountain and headed down towards where Potestas' ship lay on the beach. There was no trouble getting onto the ship. "Venaliter can't have thought ahead very well," thought Venaliter, chuckling to himself.

As he entered the ship's cabin a voice called out to him: "Who's there?"

"Geminlateral?! Is that you?" shouted Venaliter. "Where have you been? Why are you here, with Potestas on his ship?"

"I told him your plan." mumbled Geminlateral, shaking, pulling something out of his pocket. "I needed him here, so I could kill two birds with one stone. I want the hidden land. And you're not going to stop me."

Geminlateral quickly revealed the item in his pocket. He sliced off his chains using the enchanted dagger and attempted to thrust it into Venaliter. Venaliter calmly cupped his hand around the end of the blade, pulled it out of Geminlateral's hand into his own.
Geminlateral held his hands and arms over his face, shaking violently.
"Don't kill me! Please master! I have been very foolish indeed! I did not want to harm you, I just became ruled by greed and lust for power." He started to weep, and Venaliter put an arm around his shoulder for a moment to calm him down.

He pulled away.
"Get off this island now or I will kill you."

Geminlateral looked up, terrified.
"Yes sir." he responded, quickly, rushing over to fetch the small lifeboat.

Venaliter turned to leave and started to walk back up the mountain to see where Potestas was, but turned to see Geminlateral rowing the small boat out to sea. He smiled. Now Geminlateral was out of the way, he could concentrate on trying to track down Potestas. He put his hands in his pockets again. If he couldn't have the island, no-one could. He continued to make his way back up the mountain. He was bound to be able to see Potestas from there. As he got further up, he could see the rough outline of a silhouetted figure against the blazing sun. The figure turned to face him, and Venaliter stopped abruptly in his tracks.

Potestas and Venaliter stood, hands in their pockets staring at each other on the top of the mountain that overlooked the violence beginning to brew all around them. "What monster have you become?" asked Potestas. "What has changed you from my powerful and strong-willed brother into a foul corrupted beast?"

Venaliter didn't answer. A smirk crept across his mouth. He started to howl with demented laughter. He pulled out the bomb he had been hiding in his pocket.
"Why? What..." Potestas was stunned into silence.

"I can't win this battle." said Venaliter. "And if I can't have Vicir, then no-one will." He placed the bomb on the ground, and prepared to set it off.

But a single clicking noise made him stop. Venaliter turned to see Potestas' gun raised, pointing straight at his chest.
"No, no, no!" screeched Venaliter, sarcastically. He laughed again. He put his hands in the air. "Go on, shoot me. I know you

can't. You were always weak, Potestas. You can't really bring yourself to murder your own brother, can you?"

Potestas cried a single tear.
"What brother? The real Venaliter is long gone, the thing that stands before me is not my brother. My brother is already dead."

And with that, Potestas shot Venaliter straight in the heart. Horrified by what he had done, Potestas pointed the gun at himself and prepared to join his true brother in the upper levels of the spirits.

Potestas' men found the two bodies at the top of the mountain later that day, and immediately fired up two flares to show that the war that had barely begun was over. And as the flares rose higher and higher into the sky, like the two kings, they grew further and further away from each other.

"And with that, peace was restored to Miraba."
Gaudium yawned.

"Tell us another story, Mutaverat!" pleaded the boy.

The old man Mutaverat laughed.
"Another night my dear child, but not now because all good Soferei need rest."

"Was that story true?" asked Gaudium's brother, Opes.

111

"Of course, dear child, of course!" smiled Mutaverat. "I have many more stories like that one for I once used to work for a Soferex myself."
"You did?" Gaudium shouted, sitting up excitedly. "Which of them did you work for in that story?"

Mutaverat thought for a moment, then said: "I would like to believe that I worked for the Soferex who did the right thing and didn't become corrupt, but you can believe whatever you want to believe."

"Can people change into completely different people like that, Muta?" asked Opes.

"Unfortunately they can, but they can also change from a horrible person into a nice person. I myself was once a bit like Venaliter, but I realised that whilst power can corrupt you, people who see corruption coming can change themselves. I guess that's what I did when I was offered a way out and spared by my master."

"A bit like Geminlateral in the story then?" asked Gaudium.

"Yeah," whispered Mutaverat, half laughing, half crying. "A bit like Geminlateral."

He thought for a moment, then stood up.
"Now, you two must learn from Venaliter's mistakes for one day you two are to become Soferei."

He switched off the lights. "Goodnight children."